KT-417-929

THE MEDUSA PROJECT
HOSTAGE

Also by Sophie McKenzie

THE MEDUSA PROJECT 1: THE SET-UP

GIRL, MISSING
BLOOD TIES

SIX STEPS TO A GIRL
THREE'S A CROWD
THE ONE AND ONLY

And, coming soon

THE MEDUSA PROJECT
WORLD BOOK DAY SPECIAL: THE THIEF
THE MEDUSA PROJECT 3: THE RESCUE

SOPHIE McKENZIE

THE MEDUSA PROJECT
THE HOSTAGE

SIMON AND SCHUSTER

ACKNOWLEDGEMENTS: Thank you to all those readers who gave me feedback on the first chapter of *The Hostage*, as featured in the back of the first book in the Medusa Project series, *The Set-Up*. As a result of your comments, I've made some changes, which I think make it a much stronger opener – I hope you'll agree! SM

First published in Great Britain in 2010 by Simon and Schuster UK Ltd
A CBS COMPANY

Copyright © 2010 Sophie McKenzie

This book is copyright under the Berne Convention.
No reproduction without permission.
All rights reserved.

The right of Sophie McKenzie to be identified as the author
of this work has been asserted by her in accordance with sections
77 and 78 of the Copyright, Design and Patents Act, 1988.

Simon & Schuster UK Ltd
1st Floor, 222 Gray's Inn Road, London WC1X 8HB

This book is a work of fiction. Names, characters, places
and incidents are either the product of the author's imagination or are
used fictitiously. Any resemblance to actual people living or
dead, events or locales is entirely coincidental.

A CIP catalogue record for this book
is available from the British Library.

ISBN: 978-1-84738-526-0

1 3 5 7 9 10 8 6 4 2

Printed by CPI Cox & Wyman, Reading, Berkshire RG1 8EX

www.simonandschuster.co.uk
www.sophiemckenziebooks.com
www.themedusaproject.co.uk

For Simone and for Susie

Fourteen years ago, scientist William Fox implanted four babies with the Medusa gene – a gene for psychic abilities. Now dead, his experiment left a legacy: four teenagers – Nico, Ketty, Ed and William's own daughter, Dylan – who have each developed their own distinct and special skill.

Brought together by government agent, Geri Paterson, the four make up the Medusa Project – a secret, government-funded, crime-fighting force. They live under the protection of William's brother, Fergus Fox, at Fox's North London boarding school – Fox Academy – where both their abilities and role as psychic agents are secret.

1: Lex

Like I didn't have enough problems?

Nico and I were in a car, on the way to our first proper mission as the Medusa Project. We'd been trained, we'd been briefed and we'd been told why our mission was important. So why was I feeling as chewed up as the inside of my trainers after a long, sweaty run?

'Hey, babe,' Nico murmured. 'What's the matter?'

I shook my head. I'm not good at explaining stuff at the best of times, which this definitely wasn't. Anyway, Nico's totally sorted about his psychic ability. So are the others. It's just me . . .

I have visions of future events which – I know – *sounds* like it should be interesting. The trouble is, I can't control when these glimpses into the future are going to happen or what I'm going to see. My ability's completely random. And yet there I was – off on a mission that was built around *my* psychic powers.

'Are you scared about getting hurt?' Nico lowered his

voice so our driver wouldn't hear. 'Because you don't need to be . . . I'll make sure you're okay.' He smiled that chocolate-eyed, half-cheeky, half-sexy smile of his.

I smiled back, it was impossible not to. My boyfriend is the fittest thing on two legs – not that I'd tell him so.

'Thanks, you macho bighead, but I can look after myself.'

Nico's grin deepened. 'So what's up?'

'Nothing, I'm fine.' I turned away and looked out of the window. I knew if I explained my anxieties to Nico he'd just tell me I was being silly – that my abilities were as valid and useful as everyone else's. But suppose I didn't have a vision later? Suppose I never had one again? It had been nearly two weeks since I'd had my first – and only – proper precognitive experience.

Geri Paterson – she heads up the Medusa Project – had tried all sorts to bring another vision on, from getting me to focus on pictures of random strangers to sending me into a state of deep relaxation.

Nothing, so far, had worked.

The streets outside were dark, the damp pavements glistening with the rain that had fallen earlier. We were speeding through a maze of back streets somewhere in central London. Our brief was to slip inside the offices of Fostergames, a computer games software company, and hope that the surroundings prompted a vision in me. Why Geri thought that standing in the middle of an office would help me see into the future, I had no idea.

I closed my eyes, remembering what she'd said about the mission.

Two days ago the Ministry of Defence's computer firewall was breached. The hacker had access to top secret and highly valuable information. We don't yet know what he saw or why he wants it. We suspect the hacker is Damian Foster, the owner of Fostergames – but there's no proof. Hopefully, your visions will lead us to the truth.

My stomach clenched into a knot. I felt for my phone in my pocket. Right then I'd have given anything to have been able to call my older brother.

Apart from Nico, Lex is the only person in the world I can truly rely on. Our parents work abroad, so I've spent most of my life since I was eleven in boarding schools. And, until last year, Lex was always there with me, helping with everything from homework to homesickness. He's so cool. Even when he left school last summer, just before I started at Fox, he still called me all the time. Right now, I really wanted to talk to him. But Lex had been busy for the past few weeks with a new job, a new flat and a new girlfriend. I hadn't even had a chance to tell him about the Medusa gene thing. After all, it's not exactly the sort of thing you blurt out over the phone, is it?

'We're here.' Nico's voice drew me back to the present. He squeezed my hand. 'Don't worry. You'll have a vision, babe.'

I stared at him. How had he known what I was worrying about?

He raised his eyebrows. 'Busted,' he whispered. 'I know you better than you think.'

3

God, Nico's *so* gorgeous – not just his dark eyes and high cheekbones – but this way he has of looking at you from under his fringe that makes you think he's laughing and wanting to kiss you all at the same time.

Feeling my face flush red, I got out of the car. The driver was a skinny blonde woman called Maria. Geri had brought her in to help train the four of us in basic attack and defence skills. We were getting pretty good.

'Fostergames is two doors down,' Maria said quietly, handing Nico a headset. 'Mobiles switched off?'

Nico and I nodded. Suddenly the atmosphere tensed up. This was it. Nico hooked the headset round his ear.

'Right, you know the floor plan of the building,' Maria said briskly. 'Get to the Fostergames offices on the second floor. Get in. Get to work. Get out. Any problems, speak into that.' She pointed to the mouthpiece of Nico's headset. 'If you run into a security guard, you've got two minutes to get out under your own steam. After that, I'm coming in. And be discreet, Nico. You're here purely to support Ketty. Don't use your telekinesis where there are witnesses . . .'

'Yes, ma'am.' Nico shook his fringe out of his eyes and grinned.

How could he be so calm about what we were about to do? I was shaking like a leaf as we walked to the Fostergames offices. When Geri first briefed us about this mission I'd assumed all four of us would be involved at every stage, but then she'd gone on to say how she didn't want us barging into Foster's office mobhanded . . . that the point of this

4

initial investigation was for me to have a vision, with Nico along as a sort of bodyguard.

No pressure, then.

It was dark now and the streets were fairly empty. I stared into the Fostergames lobby. It was smart, with a lush red carpet and a smooth pale wood reception desk in the corner. A glass vase full of huge red roses stood on top of the desk. A bald security guard sat behind it, flicking through a magazine. I fixed my gaze on the row of CCTV monitors beside him. We were clearly visible on one of the screens – standing outside the front door.

'Ready?' Nico winked at me.

'Yes.' The word came out as a whisper.

Nico held up his hand to the glass door. I watched him closely. I'd only seen him use his telekinesis properly once before – and as I'd been falling down a cliff at the time, I hadn't been able to see exactly what he did.

Nico made a slight twisting motion with his hand. Seconds later the vase on the reception desk tipped over. Water splashed onto all the CCTV monitors and into the keyboards beneath. The glass vase rolled across the counter top and smashed out of sight. The security guard spun round, cursing.

'Go on,' Nico muttered.

As if on cue, the security guard bent down, disappearing behind the desk. A second later, all the monitors went black as he switched them off.

Nico twisted the door handle and silently opened the outer door. I crept through after him as he opened the inner door. Holding my breath, I followed Nico across the soft carpet of the lobby. The guard was still out of sight behind the reception desk, presumably still dealing with the water-logged electronics.

We scurried silently to the shelter of the corridor and along, to the stairs at the end. The whole journey from the door had taken just a few seconds. The security guard hadn't noticed a thing.

As we crept up the stairs, Nico whispered, 'Well, that was easy. The CCTV'll be off for ages.'

'Don't get cocky,' I whispered back. 'Maria wants us out of here in ten minutes.'

Nico rolled his eyes. 'Through here.' We'd reached the second floor now. Nico was pointing at a door marked *Fostergames*, which led to an open-plan office.

He pressed his finger against the headset in his ear. 'Maria's telling me to shut up and let you get a feel for the place. Man . . .' he covered the mouthpiece with his hand, 'man . . . she's bossy.'

Nodding vaguely, I went through to the office. Desks were shoved together in groups of sixes and eights – and, like the rest of the building, lit by bright overhead lights. Most of the desks were fairly messy, covered in papers and files, each one with a computer terminal. Geri's instructions rang in my ears.

Once you're inside the office, stop for a few seconds at each desk. Allow yourself to get a feel for the place.

'Why should getting a feel for the place bring on a vision?' I murmured under my breath.

'I know,' Nico whispered, covering his mouthpiece again. 'It would make more sense if Geri had told you to go to Foster's office and wait for a vision vibe there. *He's* the one they think did the hacking.'

I nodded. Undercover agents had already secretly broken into Fostergames and searched Foster's computer, finding nothing. Foster himself was under surveillance. I'd seen a picture of him, but didn't know much about the man.

I wandered from desk to desk, stopping at each one, as instructed. When I'd had a vision before it had started with a sweet smell and flashing lights.

There was no sign of either of those now.

'Anything?'

'Nope.'

Nico sighed. He held out his hand and teleported a stapler, a memory stick and a white board marker into the air. I watched the objects twirl over our heads and thought about the way Nico had knocked over that vase earlier. My visions were useless in comparison with his power to move objects without touching them. Why couldn't I have some practical, useful ability like telekinesis too?

I wandered to another desk and gazed at its contents. Then another. Still nothing.

Footsteps sounded in the corridor outside.

I froze. Nico landed the objects he'd been teleporting, grabbed my hand and tugged me behind the nearest desk. Heart pounding, I crouched down as the door opened. The security guard we'd seen earlier peered into the room. My heart was beating so loudly now, I thought he would hear it. Had Nico's telekinesis somehow attracted his attention? No, the guard was just gazing around, not looking for anything in particular. This was just a routine inspection of the kind Geri had warned us about. The guard looked round, then withdrew. As his footsteps faded away, Nico let out his breath in a sharp sigh.

'That was close,' he whispered.

I nodded. Nico turned away frowning . . . pressing his finger against the earpiece of his headset again. 'What . . .? Okay . . . okay,' he muttered into the mouthpiece. He turned back to me, making a face. 'Maria says our ten minutes are nearly up. We have to get out of here before the security guard finishes looking round upstairs.'

I stood up. 'Fine.' I wandered round a few more desks. *God*, this was hopeless. How embarrassing to have to go back and admit I'd failed. I stood at the next desk. What had Geri said?

Take a moment at each desk. You don't know what will spark off a vision.

I gazed at the contents of the next desk – a few neatly piled papers . . . a pot of pens . . . a tiny teddy propped up against the PC. Then the next . . . this one was messier, with Post-it notes scattered across the desk and a large tube of handcream shoved in a corner beside a stapler and a hole punch.

Nico pointed to a sign pinned to one of the screens that divided the desk. The notice read:

Fostergames Co is a Paper Minimising Environment.

Please minimise your usage. Only print essential items.

Across this someone had scrawled: *Please minimise your arse.*

I attempted a smile, then looked at the next desk. Another fairly messy one, with a couple of car mags visible under a huge sheaf of papers. A photograph had been Blu-tacked to the side of the computer screen. I stared at it, my stomach suddenly falling away from me.

My brother Lex was in the photo, his arm around a girl I didn't know with a snub nose and short, reddish hair.

I couldn't believe it. What was a picture of Lex doing here? I glanced at the rest of the desk . . . the car mags were exactly the sort of thing Lex would own. And then I saw the tiny, blond-haired troll, perched on the edge of the in-tray.

I'd won it at a funfair we'd been to last year. I'd been so pleased with myself and Lex had hugged me and I'd laughed and said the troll looked like him with his long, surfer-dude hair and I'd written *LW*, Lex's initials, on the troll's feet and given it to him and Lex's face had scrunched up in that gap-toothed, crooked smile of his.

I reached out and picked up the tiny troll. Hands shaking I turned it over. There, on the base, was the *LW*. Faded, but distinct.

'Ketty?' Nico whispered at my side.

I hardly heard him. Lights flashed in front of my eyes. A sweet, heavy smell filled my nostrils. It was happening again. A vision.

Rain. Stone. Leaves and ivy. Rain on my face. I'm behind a

9

large stone, hiding. Lex is just in front of me, but he doesn't know I'm there. He's holding a small silver device. A splash of rain on metal. He hands the device to another man whose face I can't see. The man speaks. 'This has the recording . . .' – his voice is low, fading as the rain gets harder, then returning – '. . . the MoD data?' And Lex says: 'Yes, it's the only copy.' I shiver, watching . . . hiding . . . rain on my face . . .

I snapped out of the vision.

'Ketty?' Nico's anxious face zoomed into focus. 'Man, what happened? Was that a vision? You, like, just zoned out for about ten seconds and now you're white as . . .' He grabbed my arm. 'Come on, we have to get out of here.'

I stared at him blankly, unable to take anything in. Nico pulled me towards him. We were so close that I could hear Maria's voice through Nico's earpiece. She was telling Nico to get me out of the building. I felt sick. Nico pulled me, stumbling, to the door.

My head spun as we raced down the stairs and past the now deserted reception desk. Nico glanced at me anxiously, then focused on the front door. We'd been warned that if the security guard went on his rounds, he would lock the outer glass door. Maria must have been hissing in Nico's ear again, because he was muttering into his mouthpiece.

He held up his hands and the door lock clicked open. I was vaguely aware of how impressive this was – a week ago there was no way Nico could have used his telekinesis on a lock – but my mind was still all-focused on what I'd just seen.

10

As we ran out, onto the pavement, the reality sank in. I'd had a vision of Lex handing someone a recording to do with the MoD data. Which meant my *brother* – not Foster, the boss of Fostergames, but my wonderful older brother – must be the hacker Geri had briefed us about!

And *I* was part of the crime-fighting force supposed to catch and stop him.

2: The secret

I don't remember much about the journey back to school. I could barely walk as we left the office block. I have this vague recollection of Nico holding me up, then Maria rushing over and bundling me into the car.

'What happened?' Maria kept saying. 'What did you see in your vision?'

But I couldn't speak.

I kept going over what I'd just seen. Lex was a hacker stealing government defence data and handing it over to . . . who? Not the police. I was sure of that.

Except none of this made sense. Lex was good with IT stuff but surely he wasn't capable of hacking into the database of a top secret government department? Then again, how would *I* know what he was capable of? I hadn't even known that his new job was with Fostergames. Lex and I hadn't talked much for the past couple of weeks. I'd been caught up with all the Medusa stuff, while Lex had sounded distracted. I'd thought it was just the new job – the new girlfriend – but now . . .

My eyes filled with tears.

'Ketty?' Nico shook my arm. We were in the back of the car now, zooming away from Fostergames. 'Please talk to me. You're acting *really* weird. What *happened*?'

Maria twisted round from the driver's seat. 'What did you see?'

I swallowed, trying hard to pull myself together. Trying to work out what to say. One thing I was sure of . . . I couldn't tell anyone what I'd seen. *Who* I'd seen. Not without talking to Lex first.

'It wasn't much,' I said, shakily. 'I saw this man hand over something to another man. I didn't see either of their faces. But the first man said he had a recording to do with the MoD data.'

Maria nodded, her thin lips pressed together. But Nico was looking at me, frowning.

'That's all you saw?' He sounded sceptical. 'Why did it make you so upset, then?'

'I don't know,' I said, turning to look out of the window. It was still raining – a light drizzle that made everything out-side – the passing cars and people and streets – seem slightly misty and unreal.

I shoved my hands deep into my pockets. With a jolt I made contact with the little troll from Lex's desk. I'd been holding it in my hand when I had the vision. I must have put it in my pocket without realising.

Our head teacher, Mr Fox, met us at the school gates. He was waiting for us, pacing anxiously up and down – his

13

huge frame filling the front path. I like Mr Fox. He's Nico's stepdad as well the head – and it's obvious how much Nico means to him. Plus I liked how he'd tried to stand up for us when Geri Paterson forced us to be part of the Medusa Project.

'What happened?' Mr Fox said. 'Are you both all right? Ketty looks pale.'

'We're fine,' Nico said.

'Though Ketty's vision has disturbed her,' Maria added. 'I need to take her to Ms Paterson straight away.'

Oh, God.

Mr Fox turned to me, his forehead creased with a frown. 'It sounds like she should be in the sick room.'

'I'll take her,' Nico volunteered.

'I don't need to go to the sick room,' I insisted. 'I'm fine.'

Mr Fox nodded, reluctantly. 'Okay. Well, Geri's waiting for you in my office. I'll come along in a moment, make sure you're all right.'

Maria took me to Mr Fox's office. Geri Paterson was perched on the arm of his big leather chair. As usual, she was smartly dressed in a suit and blouse. Her fine, sharply-cut bob swung against her chin as she looked up at me. I had no idea how old she was – older than my mum, I thought – but not slow, like most older people – there was something restless about her that made her seem young – like a bird, always pecking around for the next bit of food.

'You may go, Maria,' she said.

Maria backed out of the office and shut the door. Geri

14

smoothed an imaginary speck of dirt off the front of her jacket. 'So, what happened?' she said. Her eyes bored into me, somehow managing to look both cold and excited at the same time. 'What did you see, Ketty?'

I hesitated, then told her what I'd told Nico and Maria.

'That's it?' Geri sounded disappointed.

I nodded, feeling awkward.

'What brought on the vision?' Geri leaned forward in her chair.

I shuffled uncomfortably, thinking about Lex's desk. How I'd noticed the photo of him and the girl . . . the little troll on his in tray . . . I felt in my pocket for the tiny figure, its hair rough against my fingers. 'I'm not sure what brought it on . . .'

'Okay, what was the last thing you saw *before* the vision?' Geri persevered.

I shrugged.

Geri frowned. 'A photo perhaps?' she said. 'Of a family member?' She paused. 'A *brother*, perhaps?'

I stared at her. Her eyes were bright and hard. My mouth fell open.

'You *knew*?'

Geri sat back, laughing her thin, tinkly chuckle. 'That Alexander – Lex – works for Foster? Of course I knew. Why d'you think I was so insistent that you look at every single desk in the office.'

I gritted my teeth, unable to get my head around what she was saying. 'You mean you *wanted* me to find out he worked there while we were snooping about?'

'Of course, dear. I mean, it was obvious from your reaction during the briefing you had no idea where your brother's new job was. An opportunity, I thought. And then the agents who have the place under surveillance told me that there was a photo of your brother on his desk. I was hoping that when you saw it, it might prompt you into a vision – just as seeing Nico on that cliff top prompted the one before.'

'So you think Lex is involved in the MoD hacking?' My mind was careering wildly around different possibilities. Did Geri already suspect him?

'No, dear.' Geri flicked back her hair. 'Of course not. As you know, all the clues we have point to Foster as a loner. We know he has advanced IT skills – he was in trouble as an adolescent on hacking charges, though the case was dropped – and there are many aspects of the MoD hacker's style which echo his juvenile hacking signatures. Foster will have his reasons for what he's doing, but I doubt if they include any desire to endanger any of his employees. I just hoped the shock of seeing your brother's picture when you were already in a stressful state would . . .'

'. . . would tip me over the edge into a vision?' I stared at her. Anger settled – hard and solid – in my stomach. How *dare* Geri manipulate me like that?

'Which it did,' she said, as if that justified everything.

At that moment the door opened and Mr Fox appeared. 'I think Ketty's had enough for one day,' he said, his voice gentle but firm.

16

'Fine. Call me if you have another vision. You've got the emergency number I gave you at the briefing, haven't you?'

I nodded feeling sullen.

Geri waved me away with her hand. 'Just remember everything you've been told about Foster is in the strictest confidence, Ketty. Under no circumstances are you to tell your brother of our suspicions – you'll not only jeopardise our investigations, you may well put Lex in danger.'

I left the office in a daze. Mr Fox led me along the corridor to the stairs to the girls' dorm. He kept shooting anxious glances at me. 'Are you sure you're all right, Ketty?'

I made a huge effort trying to reassure him, pretending I was just tired. It was past curfew and Monday – a school night, so I knew there was no chance of seeing Nico again before morning. I wasn't sure I wanted to see him anyway. It felt wrong not telling him the truth, but how could I admit to what I'd seen? That Lex was the hacker . . . that at some point in the future he was going to hand the MoD information to someone for . . . well, for money, presumably . . . I could barely admit it to myself, let alone tell someone else.

I walked into the dorm. It was a big room, with four beds, a long wardrobe and a private bathroom off to the left. Of the three boarding schools I'd lived in, Fox Academy was by far the most comfortable. I'd been here since the start of the school year – when Mr Fox contacted my parents and offered me a place – and it had felt like home straight away.

Right now, though, it felt like a prison. On top of which, all three of my cellmates were in the room.

Don't get me wrong. Normally I didn't mind sharing. Most of the girls at Fox were nice enough and though I didn't have a bestie, I was kind of friends with almost everyone. Not quite all, though . . . Dylan was stretched out on her bed, flicking through one of those boring fashion magazines. As she saw me, she swung her long, slim legs round and sat up.

'You look real awful,' she drawled in her American accent.

Charming.

Right then, I wished I didn't have to share a dorm room. Especially with Dylan. I think Mr Fox hoped we'd get on or something, because of us both having the Medusa gene. I don't know what fantasy world he was living in. Dylan doesn't get on with anyone.

Noises from the bathroom. I glanced through the door, where our room-mates, Lola and Lauren, were giggling away over something. They didn't know about Medusa. No one else at school did. Just Mr Fox, Nico, Ed – and Dylan.

'I'm going for a run,' I said, reaching under my bed for my trainers. I'd only bought them the week before. Expensive Asics with an air-cushioned sole.

'Whatever floats your boat.' Dylan twisted her long red hair round her hand. She lowered her voice. 'So what happened in Foster's office?'

'Not much.' I glanced again at the bathroom in case we were being listened to, but the other girls were giggling harder now, paying us no attention. 'I just . . . I feel a bit weird . . . need some air.'

'Well don't barf over me, these are designer jeans.' Dylan turned back to her mag.

Snotty cow.

I grabbed my Asics, tied a piece of string round my hair and left the room. I slipped down the stairs and let myself out of the fire door at the back of the school, praying I wouldn't run into any of the teachers. It was almost 11 p.m. now – I'd get a detention if I was caught outside at this time.

I ran round the back of the school, past the playing fields and into the Top Field. I don't know if I can explain how amazing running is. How it calms me down. It's like . . . the first few minutes it's an effort and nothing feels quite right and then it's like the world comes into focus and your breathing steadies and you feel like you could run forever.

A few weeks ago, just at the start of the Medusa Project, I twisted my ankle and couldn't run properly for a week. It was awful. I was supposed to be running in a marathon around then, too – Nico sorted it – but it didn't happen.

I ran on now trying to focus on myself crossing the finish line of the London Marathon. But Lex and my vision was always there – a nagging anxiety in my chest. After a while I stopped and leaned against a tree. The wind was cool on the back of my neck. I took a deep breath of the crisp night air, my thoughts settling at last.

My vision suggested Lex was – or was going to be – involved in the MoD hacking. But there was only one way I could know for sure. I had to call him, no matter what Geri had said. I took my phone out of my pocket. It was nearly half-past eleven, but Lex was often up past midnight.

Hands shaking, I found his name on my contact list and pressed *call*.

3: Trust

The phone went straight to voicemail. *Damn.* I left a hurried message asking Lex to call me as soon as possible, stressing it was really important, then jogged back to the school building, still deeply troubled.

I half thought about calling Mum and Dad out in Singapore. They're our adoptive parents – they took me and Lex in after our birth mum died. Mum and Dad knew about the Medusa gene and my visions, though not about Geri Paterson's Medusa Project. But Lex and my dad don't really get on, and I didn't want my brother in any *more* trouble.

I fell into an uneasy sleep. Dylan woke me, shaking me by the arm, at 6.45 a.m. the next morning.

'Get up,' she hissed. 'We've got training with Maria in ten.'

Crap. I groaned and rolled over. Everything that had happened yesterday flooded back. I had to get hold of Lex, that was the important thing. I pulled on my sweats and followed Dylan down to the assembly hall, where we did our

21

self-defence training. As far as the rest of the school were concerned, we were getting extra help with maths.

As we waited for the others, I sent Lex a text asking him to call me when he was up. I'd try him again once our training was over.

As I finished with the text, Nico and Ed wandered in. Nico winked at me but Ed, his laptop tucked under his arm, just threw me a quick glance and a nervous half-smile. I didn't take this personally. Ed never looks people straight in the eye – he says it automatically means he reads their minds, which he *hates*.

'Hey, doofus,' Dylan sneered. 'How you doing?'

Ed shrugged. I folded my arms, annoyance burning in my chest. I hated the way Dylan looked down on Ed . . . well, the way she looked down on almost everyone. But particularly Ed. I felt bad enough about him as it was.

I guess I should explain . . .

A few weeks ago, Ed and I had sort of started going out. But then I found out that Nico, who I'd really liked all along, liked me back – so I ended things with Ed and started going out with Nico. But Ed didn't know about Nico just yet. We were keeping it secret for a bit so as not to hurt his feelings.

I know, it's complicated. And, really, the last thing I needed on top of everything else.

'Okay, guys.' Maria bounded over in her usual blue track-suit, her hair in plaits. 'Today Geri wants us to work on outthinking the opponent's attack – specifically, moving at an angle which he will *not* be expecting. So . . . let's go.' She

22

stood in front of Dylan and aimed a punch in slow motion at Dylan's stomach. 'Now, Dylan, I know you'd be able to stop this punch hurting you if you saw it coming – but how could you avoid it altogether?'

Dylan took a step back.

'See that, everyone?' Maria went on. 'The instinctive reaction we all have when we're attacked is to move away in a straight line. Either back or forward, or side to side. But what you want to do is move *diagonally*, thereby changing both your distance *and* your direction from your attacker. Let's try that again, Dylan.'

'That's enough.' Mr Fox's voice boomed from the doorway. He slammed the door shut and marched over. 'I'll take over, Maria.'

'But . . .?' Maria stared at him. 'But we've only just started. And my orders from Geri Paterson are—'

'I'll deal with Geri,' Mr Fox snapped. 'This is *my* school, Maria. And I want some time alone with *my* students.'

Maria gathered up her sports bag and flounced out. I watched Mr Fox, open-mouthed. I'd never seen him so full of barely repressed fury. The others seemed as shocked as I was. We all stood in silence, as Mr Fox gazed at each of us in turn.

We were dressed identically in the Fox Academy uniform of navy trousers and pale blue sweatshirt but, apart from that, we couldn't have looked more different. Despite the tension in the room, Nico appeared cool and relaxed. He stood, leaning against the wall, his arms lightly folded and his hair falling sexily over his eyes. Ed, on the other hand, looked awkward and embarrassed. The white shirt he wore under his sweatshirt was buttoned up to the neck and, above it, his face was flushed. Dylan, of course, somehow managed to look like a model in *her* uniform . . . She stared aggressively at Mr Fox, her hands on her hips and her face sulky.

I looked down at my own sweatshirt, noticing for the first time a red jam stain just over my left boob . . .

'Why did you send Maria away?' Dylan demanded.

'So we can work on some basic trust-building exercises,' Mr Fox said.

Nico stared at him. '*Trust*-building?'

'*What?*' Dylan's voice oozed with disbelief. 'Why?'

'The abilities you have are . . . challenging,' Mr Fox went on. 'After Ketty's experience yesterday I think it will be of more benefit to you to feel supported by each other than to learn how to handle yourselves in a fight.'

'Oh, crap,' Nico moaned under his breath. 'Man, this sucks.'

Dylan glared at me. 'Thanks a million, *lightweight*,' she muttered.

I could feel myself blushing. I looked down at the floor – wooden and covered in scuff marks from the drag of countless shoes and chairs.

Mr Fox strode up onto the stage and made us follow him with a chair each. He positioned the chairs randomly on the stage, then held out a blindfold.

'This is a basic trust exercise,' he said. 'Each person in turn will be blindfolded and asked to make their way across the stage between each of these chairs without bumping into them or falling off the stage. They won't be able to see where they're going, but another person from the group will guide them with claps. Faster clapping when they're moving too close to either a chair or the edge of the stage, slower when they're moving too far away.'

'Clapping?' Nico said, incredulously.

'This is crazy,' Dylan muttered. 'We should be practising our psychic abilities – or basic attack and defence – like we did with Maria.'

I stared at the floor.

Mr Fox held the blindfold out to Nico. 'You first.'

Nico rolled his eyes, but let Mr Fox tie the blindfold round his head. Mr Fox led him up the steps to the top of the stage, then pointed at Ed, indicating he should be the one to guide Nico across the stage.

Mr Fox spun Nico round.

'Okay . . . Go!' Mr Fox pressed down on his stopwatch.

Nico strode off. Ed clapped to guide him round each chair in turn. Nico moved confidently while Ed focused hard. Nico was across the stage in about ten seconds.

'Excellent.' Mr Fox's voice registered relief as well as pride.

Ed beamed and blushed. Nico made a face as he took off the blindfold, but I could tell he was pleased Mr Fox thought he'd done well.

Dylan chewed on one of her fingernails. 'How lame was that?' she said under her breath.

I ignored her.

Ed went next, with Dylan guiding him. He moved much more slowly than Nico, and Dylan's clapping wasn't as steady or as careful as Ed's had been. You could see she was getting impatient with him to hurry. Considering how basically uncoordinated he is, Ed made it round okay, sighing with relief as he removed his blindfold.

'Now Dylan,' Mr Fox announced.

Dylan's mouth was set in a sulky expression as he tied on her blindfold.

'Can you see anything under that?' I whispered to Nico.

'Not a glimmer,' he said.

Mr Fox pointed at me to guide Dylan with claps. I stepped over to the stage and held my hands ready, as Mr Fox spun Dylan round a few times.

'Get set . . . Go!' Mr Fox pressed his stopwatch.

Dylan took a small step forwards. Then another. I watched her intently, clapping steadily. And then she stopped. I stopped my clapping too, waiting for her to move again. But instead, Dylan tore off her blindfold.

'This is *sooo* stupid,' she said, her face almost as red as her hair. 'A big waste of time.' She pointed at me. 'And *she's* totally lame at clapping.'

She stomped down the stairs and across the hall, flinging the blindfold behind her as she left the room.

There was a stunned silence. I glanced round at Mr Fox.

He looked deeply troubled. 'That wasn't your fault, Ketty,' he said.

I opened my mouth to say *thanks . . . I know*, but Nico got there first.

'Of course it wasn't Ketty's fault,' he snapped. 'Though Dylan was right about it being a waste of time.'

I shot him a sharp look.

Mr Fox shook his head. 'What Geri is making you do – these missions – is *so* wrong. No wonder Dylan's upset.'

Nico shrugged. 'Dylan's just being a prat,' he said.

Mr Fox picked up the blindfold from the floor and held it out to me.

'Your turn, Ketty, I'll find Dylan later when she's had a chance to calm down.'

The blindfold fitted snugly. Nico had been right, you couldn't even see a glimmer of light behind it. Mr Fox's hands on my shoulders guided me up the stairs to the stage. He spun me round. Now I had no idea where either the edge of the stage or the chairs were. I swallowed, not liking how disoriented I suddenly felt.

Mr Fox's footsteps tapped away. Who was going to be clapping me through the chairs? Nico, I guessed. He was the only one who hadn't guided anyone yet.

The clapping started. Yes, it *was* Nico. I was sure of it. Ed's clapping had been softer . . . more hesitant. I stepped forwards, sure I was heading to the left of the nearest chair. Immediately the clapping sped up. My breathing quickened. I wanted to get this right . . . to do it well . . . for Nico's sake,

27

as well as mine. I turned, too hard apparently because, as I shuffled forwards again, the clapping didn't slow.

Crap. I stopped for a second trying to get my bearings, then set off again, worried the others would think I was doing a Dylan.

The clapping was *still* fast. Completely disoriented and cursing myself for being so stupid I turned sharp right. At last the clapping slowed. As it did, I smelled heavy, sweet perfume. Behind the blindfold, which just seconds before had been a blanket of black, lights dazzled in my eyes.

Rain. Stone. Leaves and ivy. Rain on my face. I'm hiding like before. Watching . . . The man with Lex examines the small silver device Lex has just given him. He looks up. My heart skips a beat. It's Foster. Lex's boss. His grey eyes are angry. Lex speaks. Softly – I can't hear him. I shiver. Rain on my face. Rain on ivy. Slippery. Stone. Foster's voice is a menacing rumble, I can't catch all the words. 'Rufus Stone . . .' he says, then, 'Killing the girl . . . only option.' He turns and I see right into his furious eyes. 'And now I'm going to have to kill you, Lex.'

'Ketty?'

'Ketty?'

I came to, disoriented. *Kill?* Kill *Lex*? My blindfold was ripped off my face. Mr Fox, Nico and Ed were standing in front of me, their faces full of concern.

I blinked, my heart racing. Foster had been talking about killing someone . . . some girl . . . and now he was going to kill Lex . . .

Kill my brother. Which meant what? That Lex was the hacker and Foster had found out? Or that Foster was the hacker after all, but that Lex was somehow involved? And who was Rufus Stone? My head spun. Whatever was going on, I had to get hold of Lex and warn him about Foster's threat. *Now.*

'I'm sorry,' I stammered. 'I just got a bit claustrophobic inside the blindfold.'

Without waiting for any of them to respond, I raced out of the assembly hall. I ran as fast as I could until I was outside by the oak tree in the Top Field.

My whole body trembled as I dialled Lex's mobile number. No reply. Again. And he hadn't responded to my earlier text, either.

I took a deep breath and left a message.

'Lex, you have to leave your job. I'll explain why when I see you, but it's Damian Foster. Your boss. He's dangerous. I . . .' I hesitated. There was no way I could explain it properly over the phone. 'Just call me back.'

I hung up. Maybe I could reach him at work. I dialled a directory to get Fostergames's number. Once through, I asked to speak to Lex Wilshere. But the receptionist said he was off sick today.

I gulped. If Lex was ill, then he should be at home. He should certainly be able to answer his phone.

I shoved my mobile in my pocket. Lex had texted me his new address a few weeks ago. A flat in Kilburn. There was only one option. I had to bunk off school and go there now.

If Lex was there, I could explain everything to him in person. If he wasn't, I could break in and try and work out where he was.

I had no idea how involved with Foster Lex already was – or what exactly Lex had done. But I was certain he was soon going to be in terrible danger. For all I knew, what I'd just seen in my vision might be only hours away from happening.

I turned back towards the school building. It was hidden from me by a line of trees. As I reached the trees, a twig cracked on the ground behind me. I spun round. The wind roared in my ears, tearing through the leaves beside me. Everything was moving. Happening so fast. So suddenly.

Out of the corner of my eye I saw it. A huge branch ripped off a tree. All wood and leaves. Hurtling through the air towards me.

I opened my mouth to scream. But no sound came out. The branch was getting closer. About to strike me. Dimly, through the leaves, I could see a figure in the distance running towards me. His yell echoed in the air.

There was no time to think. I raised my arms and waited for the blow.

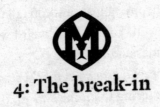

4: The break-in

Nothing happened. Silence. I realised my eyes were squeezed tight shut, and opened them cautiously.

The figure running towards me was coming so fast he was almost a blur. It was Nico, his eyes wide and terrified. I looked down. The branch that had been hurtling towards me was on the ground, just centimetres in front of me.

'Ketty, Ketty, are you all right?' Nico leaped over the branch in front of me and pulled me into a fierce hug.

'I'm fine,' I said, feeling bewildered. 'What happened? Where did that branch come from?'

Nico released me. I looked round. The wind, which had seemed to roar before, was quite still now. I stared down at the branch again.

'It was half-hanging off one of the trees. It just came away.' Nico sounded ashamed.

I frowned as realisation dawned.

'*You* did that?' I backed away from him. 'With telekinesis? *Why?*'

31

'I didn't mean to.' Nico's face was all screwed up, his eyes dark and unhappy. 'I just saw you talking on the phone out here and . . . well, you've been weird with me since we went to Fostergames and . . .'

'. . . you teleported *a branch* at me?' I stared at him in disbelief. 'You were trying to *hit* me?'

'Of course not,' Nico insisted. 'It was an accident. I felt all . . . confused and angry and I saw the branch half torn off the tree and next thing I knew it was in the air . . . It was a total mistake and I stopped it straight away.' He reached out his hand and cupped my cheek. 'You know I've always had a problem controlling my telekinesis around you. I thought I'd got that under control but . . .' He paused, stroking my cheek with his fingers.

I closed my eyes. Nothing in my life had ever felt like his hand on my face did right now. It wasn't just that my stomach was doing cartwheels and my breathing was uneven – it went to my heart, to the most fragile part of me.

I opened my eyes.

Nico smiled at me. 'I'm really, really sorry,' he said.

'It's okay,' I said, my voice all hoarse. 'I'm fine.'

Nico smiled again. There was a tiny spot to the left of his chin. A blemish on his smooth skin. Somehow it made him even more gorgeous.

You've got it bad, Ketty, said a little voice in my head.

'So who *were* you talking to on the phone?'

I could hear the angry undertone in Nico's voice. I stared at him.

32

'Don't look at me like that,' Nico said crossly. 'It's bad enough us not being able to tell people we're going out together because of stupid Ed without . . .'

'I was leaving a message for my brother, Lex. That's all.' My eyes filled with tears. I stared at the nearest tree. Its bark was rough and gnarled. Suddenly I felt about a hundred years old.

'I didn't tell the whole truth about that vision, yesterday,' I blurted out, unable to hold back the truth any longer. 'And . . . and I had another one just now in that stupid training session with Mr F— with your stepdad.

'Okay.' Nico frowned. 'What did you see?'

I took a deep breath and told him everything, including the full contents of both visions.

'So who's the girl Foster talks about killing in that second vision?' Nico's eyes grew wide. 'Ketty, suppose that's you?'

I shook my head. 'How can it be me? I've never even met Foster. He doesn't know I exist.'

'What are you going to do?' Nico said.

'I'm going to Lex's flat to see if I can find any clues as to where he is,' I said. 'Will you cover for me?'

'No, babe.'

I stared at him. Was he saying he wouldn't help me?

'Again with the look . . .' Nico grinned. 'I won't cover for you because I won't be here. I'm coming with you to your brother's place.'

I didn't argue. To be honest, I was relieved. I didn't have

33

a key, and if Lex wasn't home I'd need Nico's telekinesis to help me get inside.

We went back into school, where the teachers were taking the day's register. We answered to our names, then asked Curtis and Tom to cover for us while we skipped school for the rest of the day. They agreed, after teasing Nico a bit about us going off together. I wasn't convinced we'd get away with bunking off all day, but there wasn't time to worry about it. Finding and warning Lex was all that mattered. We changed, quickly, out of our uniforms and snuck out through the side gate.

An hour later we were standing outside a house in Kilburn. It was divided into two flats. I rang the ground-floor flat bell.

No one answered. I peered through the living room window. Empty.

'Not exactly designer, is it?' Nico made a face.

It was true. The whole house was run-down, with weeds up the path and peeling paint on the walls.

'He's only just got a job,' I said, feeling defensive.

'Any idea if he hides a spare key outside?' Nico asked.

I shook my head. 'I think we'll have to break a window,' I said uncertainly.

Nico raised an eyebrow. '*Please*,' he said. He focused on the window beside the front door. 'Watch this.'

I stared at the window. For a few seconds nothing happened then, slowly, the lock on the other side of the sash window twisted round. Nico's face was screwed up with concentration.

'Wow,' I breathed, transfixed. It was funny. My own visions were starting to feel natural, but it was still weird seeing Nico in action. 'That's *spooky*.'

The top of the lock twisted right off and dropped to the living room carpet beneath. Nico breathed a sigh of satisfaction. 'Not as spooky as your bloody predictions,' he said.

I glanced up and down the road. An old woman halfway down the street was the only person in sight.

'Come on.'

We stood side by side in front of the window and pushed the sash up. With a creak and a groan it rose. I looked round again. The old woman had turned a corner. No one was watching us.

I scrambled over the windowsill and onto the carpeted floor. The room smelled slightly musty and the furniture looked a little shabby, but it was obviously all clean – even homely, with some candles in saucers ready to light on the large wooden mantelpiece.

The huge TV that sat in the corner was, on the other hand, really state-of-the-art. Nico glanced at it admiringly as he dropped to the floor beside me.

'What do we do now?' he said.

'Have a look round,' I whispered, 'see if there's any clue to where Lex might have gone. Look for anything about Foster or that other man he mentioned in my vision – Rufus Stone.'

We crept out of the living room. A threadbare carpet ran along a narrow corridor. Two doors on the right led to a small bedroom and bathroom. Both empty. There was a kitchen at the end of the corridor. The surfaces were fairly clear – just a few plates and bowls piled in the sink. I picked up a bowl containing the remnants of some coloured cereal and sniffed. The milk at the bottom of the bowl smelled fine. Which meant Lex couldn't have been gone more than a day or so, didn't it?

'You take the bedroom,' I said to Nico. I went back to the living room. There was an old cardboard box on the floor containing some magazines and clothes. I rummaged through it, wondering what the hell I thought I was going to find.

Nothing.

A couple of minutes later, I gave up and wandered into Lex's bedroom again.

Nico was sitting on the bed, a pile of papers in his lap.

'Anything there?' I asked.

'Nothing, babe.' He made a face.

I sat down beside him and took some of the papers. Most of them were clearly irrelevant – till receipts for food and beer, some old newspapers, a scrunched up bus ticket . . . Then I picked up the blank pad of notepaper beside Lex's bed. I frowned. The top sheet of paper carried indentations. I held it up to the light. It definitely spelled something.

I grabbed my bag and took out a pencil.

Nico glanced over. 'What are you doing?'

36

I stared at him, excitedly. 'There's something written on here,' I said. 'I reckon Lex wrote something down on the sheet of paper on top of this one, then tore it off, but his writing's left markings on this piece underneath.'

Nico peered more closely. 'Yeah, you're right, but how are we going to work out what it says?'

'Look.' I held the newspaper flat and gently shaded my pencil across the indentations.

I read the words that appeared.

'*Rufus Stone, Tuesday, 5 p.m.*'

Rufus Stone . . . that was the name Foster had mentioned in my vision, earlier. My head spun. Tuesday was today – and 5 p.m. just a few hours from now.

'Whoa.' Nico sounded impressed, but my heart was sinking. I still didn't have enough information. Simply knowing that Lex was going to meet Stone today didn't help me find him. How was I supposed to know *where* they were meeting?

'So who's this Rufus Stone?' Nico peered at the note.

'Foster knows him,' I said, trying to put together all the pieces. I looked up. 'Maybe he *works* for Foster.'

'You mean like a middleman? A go-between? A way for Foster to keep his distance from Lex?'

'Maybe.' I checked the time. Almost eleven-thirty. 'Whatever's going on, we need to find out who and where Rufus Stone is, fast. He and Lex are meeting in less than five hours.'

'But how—'

A thump from the other room cut across Nico's words. It

37

was the sound of someone lurching in over the windowsill and landing heavily. A low groan followed.

Nico's eyes widened in horror.

I grabbed his arm, my heart pounding. 'Hide!' I whispered.

We ducked down behind the bed as the sound of footsteps stomped down the corridor towards us.

5: Rufus Stone

We crouched lower behind the bed.

'Maybe it's Lex?' I whispered, hoping for some miracle.

'Then why didn't he let himself in the front door?' Nico whispered back.

Oh crap, oh crap, oh . . .

'Ketty? Nico?' A familiar voice spoke, shakily, from the door.

'*Ed?*'

I peered over the side of the bed. Ed was standing by the bedroom door, rubbing his hand across his forehead. He was in his usual non-uniform outfit of polo shirt and chinos. His hair stood up in sandy tufts. As he saw me, the anxious expression on his face transformed into a smile.

'Hey, Ketty.'

'*Ed?*' Nico stood up. 'What are you *doing* here?'

'Er . . . I followed you from school. I had a couple of free periods, so—'

My mouth fell open. '*What?*'

Ed shuffled from side to side. 'You had a vision back in that training session with Mr Fox. I could *tell* and . . . I was worried about you . . . and—'

'This is typical, Ed,' Nico interrupted. 'You're always turning up wherever Ketty is, sticking your nose in. When are you going to get it through your thick head that you're not going out with her any more?' Nico clenched his fists.

Ed blushed. 'I know I'm not,' he stammered.

I put my hand on Nico's arm. 'Ed's just trying to help,' I said. 'Aren't you, Ed?'

'Of course,' Ed insisted. 'I'll help you any way that I can. I mean it. *Any* way . . .'

I stared at him. Was Ed talking about *mind-reading*? I knew how much he hated using his Medusa abilities. 'You're really prepared to—'

'Yes.' For a split second, Ed almost caught my eye. Then he looked away.

I could feel my face reddening. All sorts of emotions flooded through me. It was Nico I liked – it had always been Nico, right from my first day at school when I saw him laughing across our form room – but there was something about Ed that I'd never felt with anyone ever. Except Lex, of course. Some way Ed understood me . . . was there for me, without asking for anything in return.

'Thank you.' I held out the notepaper with the indented words I'd shaded over. 'We have to find Lex. I think he's going to meet this guy, Rufus Stone, this afternoon. But we don't know who Stone is or how to find him.'

'Ed isn't going to know some random bloke,' Nico muttered. His face was sullen.

I swallowed. Was Nico jealous of Ed? That was crazy. Ed was like a brother to me, but it was Nico I *liked*. *Surely* Nico could see that?

Ed took the scrap of paper and studied it.

'Have you heard of him?' I said. 'It's just we don't have much time.'

Ed frowned. 'The name seems familiar,' he said. 'I can't remember when or why, though.'

'Well, that's helpful.'

'Stop it, Nico.'

'I'll check on my laptop.' Ed drew a slim computer out of his bag and sat on the bed.

Nico and I glanced at each other. He rolled his eyes, then turned away. He reached out his hand towards a dented ping-pong ball in the corner of the room. It sped across the carpet then flew into his palm. Nico focused on the ball, mentally sending it zooming round the room. I knew he was calming himself down and left him to it.

Seconds passed. Ed was still poring over his laptop.

'Anything?' I said eventually.

'I'm just piggybacking on someone's wifi,' Ed explained. 'There. Now I'm online. Give me a minute.'

I wandered into Lex's kitchen. How could my big brother be mixed up in some kind of criminal hacking activity? Lex had always been so honest. So insistent with *me* about being honest.

41

My heart raced. Darkness. A strong, sweet scent. The edges of a vision . . . snatches of a vision.

Lex standing in the rain. Cold stone against my hand. Ivy . . . a gun, glinting wet.

It ebbed away. The kitchen was back.

'Ketty?' Ed was calling from the other room.

I raced across the hallway. 'What?'

Ed looked up at me, a smile on his face. Nico stood, staring over his shoulder, the ping-pong ball lying forgotten on the bed.

'*What?*' I said again.

'I *knew* I'd heard the name Rufus Stone before,' Ed said triumphantly.

'Who is he?' I asked.

'Not "who" but "where",' Ed explained. 'Rufus Stone isn't a person. It's a place.'

I scrambled to my feet. 'A *place?*' I walked over to the computer.

'It's a stone that shows where some king got killed.' Ed pointed to the screen. A picture of a tall black stone covered with writing sat in the middle of some olde-worlde style website.

The Rufus Stone is named after King William II and marks the place where he was shot and killed by an arrow – whether accidentally or purposefully is unknown.

I stared at the stone. My heart skipped a beat. 'I think this stone might be in my vision,' I said, remembering the stone in the rain I'd seen before. 'Except when I saw it there

42

were lots of other stones nearby and some were covered in ivy.'

'Maybe there *are* other stones near this Rufus Stone place,' Nico suggested.

Ed wrinkled his nose. 'Maybe, or maybe Ketty's vision was just of a different meeting.'

'No.' I paced across the room. 'It must be the same place. It makes sense now. Lex is going to hand something over to Foster and Foster is going to kill him.' Panic rose inside me again. 'And it's all going to happen this afternoon unless I stop it!'

Silence. Nico frowned. 'But Foster and your brother live in London – and they work in the same office,' he said. 'Why would they be meeting in the middle of the countryside?'

'Maybe the whole point was to get out of the city – away from anyone who might recognise them.' I sat beside Ed and peered intently at the information around the picture of the stone on the site he had found. 'The Rufus Stone is in the New Forest,' I said. 'Lex and I used to go there on holiday, to this caravan park. Every year 'til my nan died. Lex knows that area well. It's the perfect place for him to arrange a meeting.'

'But you can't be certain . . .' Ed started. 'Er . . . I mean why would he write down the details of a meeting that *he's* arranged?'

'I don't know,' I sighed. 'I don't *know* anything for sure. I'm acting on hunches and visions but the general level of weirdness in my life at the moment is so huge that this is, like, my best shot for finding Lex.'

43

'So how do we get to Rufus Stone?' Nico rubbed his hands together.

'The bus from Victoria coach station – that's how Lex and me used to go down, then my nan would pick us up from Ringwood. I guess we'll have to get a taxi from the coach stop out to this Stone.' *Crap*. This was going to be expensive. I glanced at Nico.

He shook his head. 'Sorry, babe, I've only got a few quid.'

'I've got plenty left over from my birthday last month.' Ed shoved his hand in his pocket and drew out a wodge of notes.

'Are you sure?' I asked.

'Course.'

As it turned out, Ed didn't come with us. Geri sent him a text as we were walking from Lex's flat to the tube station.

Am coming to school this afternoon. I need you for a special project. Meet in Mr Fox's office after morning classes.

'I have to head back to school,' Ed sighed. 'If Geri arrives and I'm not there, she'll be furious. And if she finds out you two aren't there either . . .'

'It's too late to worry about that now.' I smiled at him. 'Come with us. Nico and I have already skived.'

Nico sent a stone skittering across the pavement using telekinesis. 'Somehow I don't think skiving off is Ed's style,' he muttered. 'Plus he's right, if Geri works out we're not at school she'll have the police looking for us in five minutes flat.'

Ed grinned sheepishly. 'If anyone asks, I'll tell them I've seen you in the school grounds.'

'Thanks.' I smiled gratefully at him. I knew what a big deal lying and going against authority was for Ed.

As he sloped off, Nico gave a snort. 'Thank goodness he's gone.'

I rolled my eyes. 'Get over yourself, Nico, he was only trying to help.'

Nico stopped in his tracks. 'Help himself to you, you mean.'

We stood, staring at each other for a second. My stomach twisted into a knot. I hated it when Nico got angry like this.

'He's my *friend*,' I said.

Nico shook his head. 'You sure that's all? Because you promised you'd tell him we were going out together once we'd done our first mission, remember? But we've just spent most of an hour with him and you didn't mention it.'

I thought back to our conversation from a couple of weeks ago. It was true, I had promised to explain the situation to Ed, but since the mission yesterday I hadn't given it a single thought. Anyway, surely Nico could understand that finding and warning Lex was more important?

'Is that what this is about – you're jealous because I haven't told Ed we're together?'

'You haven't told *anyone*,' Nico said. 'And, you know what, Ketty, I'm starting to wonder if that's what's really

45

going on here – you not wanting *anyone* to know you're going out with me. Not just Ed.'

I shuffled uncomfortably. The sun came out and I lifted my hand to shade my eyes from its glare. Was that true? *No.* Of course, it wasn't. I'd just felt guilty about upsetting Ed.

'I'll tell Ed and everyone as soon as we get back to school.'

Nico pursed his lips. His eyes were hard. 'Promise?'

I put my arms round him. 'Promise. Now let's get down to Victoria.'

Nico nodded, his eyes softening. We turned into the tube station.

'You know who *would* be useful to have with us?' he said.

'I suppose you mean Dylan?' I shoved my hands in my pockets. A few weeks ago I'd been convinced Nico really liked Dylan. He'd insisted he didn't, but I still wasn't completely sure. I mean, she *was* really fit – all the boys at school thought so.

Nico prodded my arm. 'Now who's jealous?'

'I'm not—'

'Oh, yeah?' Grinning, Nico grabbed me round the waist. I laughed and tried to push him away, but Nico pulled me closer, tugging me with him through the barrier. The ticket checker strode towards us, but Nico teleported his clipboard onto the ground. As the ticket guy bent down to pick it up, Nico and I fled, giggling, for the escalators.

'You shouldn't do stuff like that,' I laughed as we tumbled into a train.

'Made you forget about your brother for a few seconds, didn't it?' Nico put his hands on my cheeks and lowered his face to mine. 'It's good to see you smiling, Ketts.'

I looked into his deep brown eyes. Somewhere inside me I shivered. The feelings I had for Nico were just so big . . . so scary. Suppose he didn't feel the same way back? I mean, he might be all pissed off because he was having to lie about going out with me, and maybe he *didn't* like Dylan, but that didn't mean he really cared about *me*. Part of me wanted to ask him for reassurance, but the idea of talking about my feelings was the scariest thing of all. So I just smiled.

Three hours later and I wasn't smiling any more. Neither was Nico. We'd found a coach to Ringwood easily enough, and then a taxi to the Rufus Stone from there. But as we drove through the New Forest countryside, the sky clouded over and we both fell silent.

Clouds meant rain. And there had been rain in my vision. According to the note we'd found, Lex was meeting Foster in just over an hour. Which meant Foster was about to attempt to kill Lex. And Nico and I were the only ones who could stop that murder from happening.

'Don't worry, Ketts.' Nico squeezed my hand. 'We've got my telekinesis. Lex'll be fine.'

I bit my lip, remembering the gun I'd seen in my snatch of a vision earlier today. Would Nico's telekinesis be enough against that gun? I glanced upwards. The clouds were definitely darkening. The sky felt low – like it was pressing down on us. Rain couldn't be far away.

The Rufus Stone was virtually deserted. Just an elderly couple wandering back to the car park.

'Where's the stone?' I said.

Nico pointed to a black pillar in the centre of a clearing, opposite the car park. It was just a little shorter than me – and inscribed on three sides. The writing was all old-fashioned – something about that king Ed had mentioned earlier. I was too anxious to pay much attention to the details but I was sure this wasn't the stone from my vision.

'We can hide behind that.' Nico indicated an oak tree surrounded by brambles.

I checked the time. Twenty minutes until Lex was due to meet Foster.

We made our way over to the tree as the first drops of rain fell and the elderly couple hurried into their car and drove off.

'So . . . does this place look familiar?' Nico asked.

I huddled under my jacket, trying to avoid snagging it on the brambles and holly that surrounded the oak tree. The ground by the tree was squelchy underfoot. 'Not really,' I said. 'I mean there was a stone with writing on it, but not the same one, and there was rain too, but more of it and more leaves and stuff . . . then again, it's hard to be sure . . . everything happened so fast in the vision.'

'Look.'

I followed Nico's gaze towards the path that led back to

48

the main road. A smart red sports car was zooming down towards us.

'That must be Foster,' I said.

We shrank back behind the tree. The rain was still drizzling as the car screeched to a stop. I peered between the leaves, waiting.

A girl got out of the car. She had cropped reddish hair and was wearing a smart, fitted suit and high heels that sank into the ground as she walked.

I frowned. It was the girl from the photo on Lex's desk. What was she doing here?

'No *way* is that a man in disguise,' Nico whispered, his eyes glued to the girl as she picked her way across the grass.

'Ssssh.' I prodded him.

As the girl reached the stone, a motorbike roared along the path. Lex! He got off and raced over to the girl. My heart thudded. He was considerably taller than her – and much scruffier, in jeans and a faded jacket.

They started talking. I strained – unsuccessfully – to hear what they were saying.

'I'm moving closer,' I whispered.

'Wait.' Nico tried to grab my arm, but I was already creeping away, using the massive holly bush in front of me as cover.

The ground was soft, my feet silent against the leaves underfoot. I tucked myself in behind the leaves. I *still* wasn't close enough. I peered through the leaves, pulling back one of the branches. The movement unbalanced me. I stumbled sideways, losing the cover of the holly bush for a second. I put out my hand to break my fall.

A twig snapped.

The girl and Lex spun round.

Crap.

Lex took a step forward, then faltered. 'Ketty?' he said, his eyes wide with astonishment. 'Is that you?'

6: Rainbow

'What are you doing here?' Lex sounded incredulous.

I hesitated for a second, then, praying Nico would stay hidden, I walked towards the Rufus Stone. The girl standing beside Lex stared at me, her mouth open. She was pretty – far prettier than in her picture. She had to be Lex's girl-friend, but why was he meeting her here? And where was Foster?

As I reached the Rufus Stone, the rain stopped and the sun came out. I stood, letting this detail sink in. No rain. No Foster. And a different stone. This *couldn't be* the meeting I'd seen in my vision. That, clearly, was yet to come.

I smiled nervously at Lex.

'Who's this?' said the girl.

'My sister, Ketty.' Lex turned to me. 'How did you know where I was?'

'Didn't you get any of my messages?' I said, my heart beating furiously. 'Why didn't you call me back?'

Lex bit his lip. 'I know I've been crap the past couple of

51

weeks. I saw you'd called last night. To be honest, I haven't even listened to your message yet . . . I'm sorry, but things have been really heavy . Stuff I can't explain. But why are you here? How did you even know where I was?'

I thought fast. Now was not the time to start explaining about the Medusa gene and my weird, uncontrollable visions.

'Never mind that now.' I reached up and whispered in his ear. 'You're in danger. Your boss – Foster – he's going to . . . to hurt you. You have to get away. Right now.'

'*What?*' Lex drew back, frowning.

'What the hell's going on, Lex?' The girl folded her arms and tutted impatiently. 'I haven't got all day.'

Lex glanced at her, a look of longing in his eyes. 'Please, Tessa, just give me a moment . . .' He turned to me. 'I don't know what you think you know about Foster,' he said. 'But Tessa is a journalist. A reporter with the *Hampshire Sun*.'

A *journalist*? What was Lex doing with a journalist? 'I thought she was your girlfriend,' I said.

'She was . . .' Lex blushed. 'It's hard to explain . . . the important thing is that I found something out at work and I wanted to tell Tessa, so—'

'For God's sake, Lex, what's your sister doing here?' Tessa's face scrunched into a frown. 'I agreed to meet you – I even chose this out-of-the-way place – because you said you had some major piece of information for me. I didn't think I was going to witness a bloody family reunion on top.'

'Ketty's got nothing to do with why I'm here,' Lex said, firmly.

Tessa raised her eyebrows. 'Of course she doesn't, she's a *schoolgirl*.'

I clenched my fists. 'I'm—'

'Don't, Ketts.' There was a warning note in Lex's voice.

I shut up, fuming. If Tessa had been Lex's girlfriend, then he was well shot of her. Rude cow. I looked round. Nico was still well hidden behind the oak tree. Apart from Tessa's sports car, the car park was empty.

'So tell me what you've got on Foster,' Tessa said, suddenly brisk.

'Okay.' Lex threw me a glance, as if warning me to keep quiet while he spoke. 'It was yesterday morning and I'd just got to the car park below the office. I saw Foster get out of his car. There's a hut right beside the motorbike area. He walked over to it and I was a bit late and didn't want him to see me, so I hid round the back of the hut . . . Anyway, this other man was inside. I don't know who, but I could just make out him and Foster talking . . . They were having a conversation about how Foster had hacked into the Ministry of Defence database and found something he wanted the other man to steal.'

'*Really?*' For the first time, Tessa looked interested.

'I had my phone with me so, when I heard them talking about the MoD, I recorded the rest of their conversation.' Lex held out his mobile. 'It's on here.'

I stared at the phone. It was sleek and silver. With a jolt I realised it was the device I'd seen in my vision. The one I'd seen Lex handing to Foster. Except . . . my heart leaped. I'd got it wrong. Lex wasn't the hacker. And he wasn't in league with Foster either.

He was trying to expose him.

'I'll Bluetooth the recording I made to you,' Lex went on.

Tessa nodded. She opened her bag and took out her own phone. She seemed to have forgotten I was there, all her attention fixed on Lex's mobile as he sent the recording across.

What did you record Foster saying?' Tessa asked.

'I don't know exactly. I think he's planning to steal something . . .' Lex switched on the recording. 'Listen.'

'. . . *the MoD location* . . .' It was Foster's voice. I recognised it from the visions.

'*That's where the Rainbow is?*' This was the other man. His voice was rougher and deeper than Foster's. '*Where do I take it when I've got it?*'

'*I'll leave the schematic in the usual place.*' Foster again. '*Call me when you're set.*'

'*Yes, sir.*'

The recording ended.

'Is that it?' Tessa sounded incredulous. 'What's "The Rainbow"?'

'I don't know.' Lex bit his lip. He suddenly looked very vulnerable.

'What's a schematic?' I asked.

'You told me you had *evidence*,' Tessa went on, as if I

hadn't spoken. 'Something that would get me a lead story. Not just on the *Hampshire Sun* – but something that would get me noticed . . . that I could take to a national paper. That recording doesn't even make sense. This Rainbow could be *anything*.'

'I know, but they were talking about the MoD database before I started recording and you could find out about the Rainbow, couldn't you?' Lex said desperately. 'That's why it's called *investigative* journalism. It's a big story, Tessa. Exactly the sort of thing you said you needed . . . you know, to be noticed.'

Tessa rolled her eyes. 'For God's sake, Lex, I don't even know if that's really Foster's voice.'

'It *is*.' They both looked at me.

'And how would *you* know?' Tessa asked.

'I saw him in a vision.' The words were out of my mouth before I could stop them.

Tessa stared at me as if I was completely mad. 'A *vision*?'

Lex groaned. 'Ketty, *please* . . .'

Crap. 'Forget that,' I said. 'The point is I'm sure Lex is right.'

Lex took Tessa's elbow and drew her to one side. They started talking in low voices. I glanced back at the tree where Nico was hiding and smiled to reassure him everything was okay.

And it was, sort of. I mean, at least now I knew Lex was trying to expose Foster, not collude with him. The meeting I'd seen between them in my vision *hadn't* taken place here.

It was clearly still in the future. Which meant if I could just get Lex to give *me* that phone of his, maybe I could change the future – ensure that the meeting between Lex and Foster never happened at all.

I went over to where Tessa and Lex were arguing. Lex glanced round as I approached. Tessa didn't appear to see me.

'This is about us, isn't it?' She glared at Lex. 'When I told you to be more ambitious, I didn't mean you should make up some crazy story about your boss to try and get me back.'

'I didn't make it up. I—'

'I told you last week. It's over.' Tessa stood back, her hands on her hips.

I stared at them, shocked. So *that* was it . . . Lex was hoping to win Tessa back by giving her information on Foster that she could turn into a big news story.

'Please, Tessa. I'm *not* making it up about Foster,' Lex insisted.

'He really isn't,' I added. 'Foster is involved in—'

'Shut up!' Tessa shouted.

'Hey,' Lex protested.

'For God's sake, Lex, are you telling me your crazy kid sister is the only person you could find prepared to back up your crazy made-up story?' Tessa was yelling now. 'You're pathetic.'

She shoved her phone into her handbag and stomped back to her car.

'Tessa!' Lex called.

But Tessa sped up, her heels clacking against the rough stone path. A second later she had reached her car and zoomed away.

I looked down at Lex's hand. He was still holding his silver phone, containing the original recording.

'It's okay,' I said. 'We can take what you recorded to . . . to the police.' I really needed to get the phone to Geri Paterson, but the police could do that. 'They'll make sure you're safe.'

'No, I have to go after Tessa. Make her believe me.'

'You can't. Foster is after you. He wants to kill you.' My voice rose in panic.

'You don't know what you're talking about. I don't understand how you know *any* of this, but Foster doesn't even know I overheard him talking about this Rainbow thing.' Lex was already running away from me. 'Don't you see? I've just made things worse between me and Tessa. I *have* to make her see I've got a real story for her. *Then* we can go to the police.'

I raced after him. 'Wait.'

Lex reached his motorbike and picked up his helmet. I turned, desperate.

'Nico, help!'

Nico darted out from behind his tree and raced towards us. Lex did a double take.

'Who on earth—?'

'That's Nico,' I said. 'My . . . er . . . my boyfriend.' I blushed. I'd never said those words before, about anyone.

Lex stared at me. 'Really? Good. Then he can make sure you get back to school okay.' He fished in his pocket for some money and shoved some notes into my hands. 'I'm sorry I don't have a spare helmet for you or I'd drop you somewhere, but I *have* to go after Tessa and straighten this mess out. Please phone a taxi. Get on a train back to London. *Please*.'

'No . . .'

'I'll call you later.' And with that, Lex jammed his helmet on his head and sped off so fast he nearly collided with a large blue Mercedes driving towards the car park. The car swerved to avoid him, its wheels spinning into a ditch.

Nico raced up, panting, as the car revved, desperately trying to back out of the ditch. 'What happened?'

I explained, my voice faltering as I spoke. 'And now Lex is gone and he's still got the recording and Foster is out there and—'

'It's okay, Ketts.' Nico smiled. 'All we have to do is call Geri. Get her to get the police to pick him up.'

Behind us, the driver of the blue Mercedes got out of his car. But I wasn't looking at him. My whole focus was on Nico.

'That's a *brilliant* idea.' I hugged him.

'Course it is,' Nico grinned. 'I mean, I hate having to do it in a way, but we need Geri's help. And it's okay now. I mean, she won't like Lex trying to give the Rainbow infor-mation to a journalist, but it's not as if he's actually involved in what Foster is planning. I bet *we* won't be in trouble

58

either, even though we skived off school. Not once Geri hears about this Rainbow thing Foster wants to steal.'

I looked up the track towards the main road. The man from the blue Mercedes had turned away from his car and was looking in our direction. For a few seconds I didn't recognise who it was.

And then the man started walking towards us. His angry grey eyes fixed on me, his face set in a snarl.

Foster.

My heart seemed to stop beating. Beside me, Nico stiffened.

Foster stared at us. Something metallic was in his hands. It glinted in the sun.

'Oh crap.' Nico grabbed my hand . . . pulling me closer towards him.

I stared at what Foster was holding, my brain taking a few seconds to catch up with my eyes.

And then I realised. It was a gun.

7: The gun

Foster was taller than I'd imagined from my vision. Thickset too, with intense grey eyes and wavy hair that curled onto the collar of his open-neck shirt. His expression was chillingly calm as he pointed his gun at us. 'Off the path. Into the trees,' he ordered.

I caught Nico's eye as we stumbled through the bushes. He looked more scared than I'd ever seen him.

Once under the cover of the trees, Foster pointed us to stand a metre or so away from him. He held the gun out towards me.

'I saw you talking with Lex before he bloody ran me off the road. Who are you? Why were you meeting him?'

My mouth fell open. How had he found us?

'Who's Lex?' Nico said.

He sounded completely genuine, but Foster just shook his head.

'You can skip the lies,' he snarled. 'I know Lex has been spying on me. I saw him on our office car park CCTV . . .

looked like he was recording something on his phone. And I hacked his texts earlier. He was meeting someone here . . . Tessa . . . is that you?'

'No. He wasn't . . . he didn't . . .'

'I saw you together.' Foster's voice was low and deeply threatening. 'And it looked like he was leaving in a hurry. He didn't even *see* my car on that bike of his. What happened? What did he tell you?'

I didn't know what to say. My eyes fixed on the gun in Foster's hand.

'*Speak.*' Foster cocked the gun and took a step closer to me.

'This is Ketty,' Nico said quickly. 'She's Lex's sister. She's not the person he came here to meet.'

Foster frowned. He lowered the gun a fraction. 'His sister? Why did he want to see you?'

'He didn't,' I said, trying to keep my voice steady. 'I followed him . . . I just wanted to see *him* . . . he's my brother . . .'

'You're lucky you *can* see your brother.' Foster's voice had a bitter edge. 'I haven't been able to see mine properly for two years.'

I shook my head. What was he talking about?

'Don't mess me around, Ketty,' Foster snarled. 'I know Lex spied on me and then came here to meet someone. I saw the two of you together. What did he say? Did he give you something?

My legs shook. I suddenly remembered the girl Foster

had mentioned in that second vision. The one whom killing was the 'only option'.

Nico had been right. That *was* me, wasn't it?

'Just give me whatever Lex gave you and you can go.' Foster levelled his gun at me.

Nico gripped my hand.

I swallowed. 'Seriously, we don't have—'

'*Now*,' he said.

I turned to Nico. Our only chance was his telekinesis. I was sure Foster didn't know anything about that. I could see from Nico's expression he knew what he had to do. He gave me a slight nod.

'Mr Foster . . .' he began.

'This isn't a discussion—'

Wham.

With a sudden upward jerk of his hand, Nico teleported Foster's gun up, out of his hand and away, into the bushes. A twist of Nico's other wrist and Foster himself stumbled, losing his footing and falling onto his side on the soft ground.

'Run!' Nico grabbed my wrist. We dived through the trees and out into the car park. We turned left and raced up the track that led back to the road.

Nico was running fast, almost dragging me after him. I found my feet. Sped up. One thing I know how to do is run. I dug into the ground with my heels, propelling myself forwards.

A roar behind us. Foster. Nico darted sideways into the

trees. He let go of my hand as we flew across the dropped leaves, weaving in and out of brambles and bushes and more trees.

'Come here!' Foster sounded close.

Nico glanced over his shoulder. 'This way.'

He tugged me with him, through a thick clump of trees. Together we burst out, onto the main road. Cars were zooming past.

Panting, Nico held out his hand, thumbing for a ride. I looked over my shoulder. I could hear Foster crashing through the undergrowth, though I couldn't see him.

'Come on, stop!' Nico shouted at the traffic. His face was screwed up, red and sweaty. He looked insane.

'Let me do this.' I pushed his raised arm down and stood in front of him. I raised my hand. Two cars passed. Then a third slowed to a standstill beside us.

An elderly lady leaned out. 'This is a dangerous place to stop,' she said. 'Does your mother know you're out here?'

'Yes,' I lied, trying to stay calm – we didn't have time for questions. 'We were supposed to meet her in Ringwood, but we got off at the wrong bus stop.'

The elderly lady frowned. 'Well, you'd better get in . . .' She looked past me at Nico. 'Is that your friend?'

'Er . . . yes,' I blushed.

'All right. You can both get in. I'm going to Ringwood anyway.'

We scrambled into the back of her car. As she sped off I

looked out the back window in time to see Foster emerging from the trees just metres from where we'd been standing. He looked round wildly. I was certain he didn't spot us.

'That was close,' I whispered.

Nico nodded. He sat back against the seat, shaking his head.

'How come you didn't see *that* in your visions?' he muttered.

I shook my head, still trembling. I would have liked the answer to that question myself.

'What are your names?' the elderly lady asked. 'Have you two been to school today?'

Nico answered, spinning some entirely convincing lie about our teachers having a training day. I could barely follow what he was saying. I was counting the seconds until we reached Ringwood and were free to call Geri.

A few minutes later the lady dropped us at the coach stop. As Nico studied the timetable for buses to London, I rang Geri. I told her I'd had another vision of Lex at the Rufus Stone and followed him down here. She was shocked. *Really* shocked . . . That I'd had the vision. That Nico and I had gone off on our own. That my brother was involved. That Foster had been carrying a gun . . .

She was particularly interested, of course, in Lex's recording about the Rainbow.

I told her everything – except that Lex was trying to give the recording to a journalist. I knew Geri wouldn't like that

64

and I didn't want him to get into trouble. I made out Lex only ended up at the Rufus Stone because he was in a panic, running away from London. That it was a random destination.

At Nico's suggestion I also pretended that we'd been forced to act independently because we couldn't get hold of Geri earlier. She tutted at this, asking quite reasonably why we hadn't gone to Mr Fox or Maria instead, but said a proper debrief (or 'telling off', as Nico translated) could wait until we were back at school.

'Foster knows my full name now,' I said. 'D'you think he'll be able to find out where I live?'

'Not a chance,' Geri said. 'There's no network access to Fox Academy's school records. As soon as you're back at school we'll make sure your surname and any identifiable pictures are taken off the other online presences you have.' Geri paused. 'The important thing now is getting you back safe.'

It turned out there was a coach to London due in a couple of minutes. Geri told us to get on that, and that she'd send Maria to meet us at Victoria station.

'And you'll get someone to find Lex?' I asked.

I could hear Geri's pen tapping against her desk.

'I'll have the police pick him up asap,' she said briskly.

'Please hurry. I'm worried about Foster reaching him first.'

Geri reassured me and rang off. I tried to call Lex myself, but his phone was switched off. I couldn't even leave a message.

The coach was hot and stuffy. Nico fell asleep after a while, his head lolling against my shoulder.

I gazed out of the window. The sun was setting to the left of the motorway – a low orange disc in a now clear pink sky. I suddenly felt terribly alone. Why did I have this curse of a psychic ability? My visions were too random to be helpful . . . all that time I'd wasted thinking Rufus Stone was a person . . . then assuming it was the place where Lex was meeting Foster. I kept getting it wrong, over and over . . . and now Lex was in serious danger and I couldn't even help him.

A tear trickled down my face as I stared out at the passing trees. For the first time I truly understood why Ed hated his ability so much.

'What is it, Ketts?' Nico's voice was soft and concerned. He turned my face towards his. 'Why are you crying?'

'I hate having visions,' I wept. 'I hate what I see. I hate not knowing when it will happen. I don't even know whether or not I can change things once I've seen them. I *hate* it.'

I sobbed into his chest for a minute, then pulled away to blow my nose.

As I wiped my eyes, Nico held my face in his hands. For a second all I could feel was the softness and strength of his fingers. The hugeness of how much I felt for him pulsed through me again. It was overwhelming. Terrifying.

'Let me help you, Ketts,' he whispered.

I nodded, barely trusting myself to speak. 'How?' I whispered back.

Our faces were centimetres apart. His eyes were gentle and chocolate brown. Melting me.

'I've got an idea.' Nico's beautiful face slid into a smile. 'I'll show you once we're back at school . . .'

8: Visions

It was hours before Nico and I were finally on our own together. Geri and Fergus were waiting for us when Maria delivered us back to school.

As soon as we got out, Fergus whisked Nico away and Geri took me into an empty classroom. She sat at the teacher's table, arms folded, her thin, lipsticked lips pressed disapprovingly together.

'This won't do, dear,' she said crisply. 'I can't have you running off on your own, it's too dangerous. And I can't keep coming up to Fox Academy to see you – not every day. That's why you have my phone number, so that you can reach me – and Maria here, posing undercover as a tutor.'

'But we tried to reach you . . .' I lied. 'And . . . and it was Lex . . . my brother was in trouble . . .'

'All the more reason to let me help.' Geri flicked back her blonde bob. 'Believe me, I want you to use your abilities. But not without back-up.' She paused. 'Anyway, I think you'd better start from the beginning again. What happened?'

I repeated what I'd told her – Nico and I had gone over our stories before reaching London to make sure they matched up. We were basically telling the truth about everything except Tessa Marshall. Nico had agreed straight away that Lex would be in trouble if Geri knew he'd been talking to a journalist, so went along with my decision not to mention her. When Geri asked why I thought Lex had made the Rainbow recording, I told her that he'd originally intended to take it to the police, but was now too scared of Foster to do so.

Geri interviewed me for about thirty minutes, then let me go – after extracting a promise from me that I would never again act without consulting her and promising, for her part, that the police were doing all they could to find Lex. I'd tried his number again, but now all I got was a recorded message saying the phone service had been discontinued.

'Something must have happened to him,' I said to Nico when we finally met up later that evening in the common room.

'Not necessarily. In fact it's a good sign,' Nico said. 'Lex has probably realised he can be tracked through his phone, so he's got rid of it.'

This sounded plausible, though it didn't stop me worrying. If I could only bring on a vision I might be able to find out where Lex was. I was about to ask Nico what he'd meant earlier when he'd said he could help me, but Fergus came into the common room and shooed us off to bed.

We met again straight after breakfast. The Tranquillity Garden is a small, walled patch of grass with rows of rose beds beyond. It's totally private, being neither overlooked nor en route to any of the major school buildings, and, because there's a rule about being silent there, it's hardly ever used.

It was certainly empty at 8.20 a.m. that Wednesday morning.

I wasted no time. 'So what's your idea for helping with my visions?'

Nico teleported a pebble from the ground and made it spin round his wrist.

'There are some techniques that might give you a bit more control over them,' he said. 'Not that rubbish Fergus was getting us to do with stupid trust exercises, but some of the stuff Jack Linden showed me.'

I stared at him. Jack Linden was the man who was responsible for both of us nearly dying just a few weeks ago. The man who'd worked for Geri, tracking us all down, then trying to sell us – and the formula for the Medusa gene – to another criminal.

'Jack Linden?'

'I know he was a conman,' Nico said quickly, letting the pebble fall to the ground. 'But he knew what he was talking about when it came to helping me get a handle on my telekinesis. Maybe some of what he suggested would help you control when and how you have your visions.'

I nodded. It was worth a try. 'Show me.'

I sat on the wooden bench by the rose beds. Several of the plants were full of dark green leaves and tight buds. None were in bloom, yet.

Nico made me close my eyes and take some deep breaths. 'What happens just before a vision?' he asked.

'I see flashing lights and I smell a sweet, heavy perfume smell.'

'Okay.' Nico hesitated. 'Imagine those now.'

I frowned. How was I supposed to do that? I tilted my face so that I could feel the sun on my closed eyelids. The light was bright now, but not flashing. In my mind's eye I imagined the light moving. Nothing happened. I shook my head.

'Try blinking,' Nico suggested.

I started opening my eyes a fraction, then closing them again. Faster and faster. It gave the impression of flashing lights.

My heart raced, as the sight I was creating triggered a surge of adrenalin.

'Now the smell,' Nico reminded me.

I kept blinking, trying to pretend that a sweet heavy smell was filling my nostrils. I suddenly realised how ridiculous I must look. My eyes snapped open. Nico was squatting in front of me, staring intently at me.

'What happened?' he said.

'I just . . .' My face flushed with embarrassment. 'I stopped because I thought I must look really stupid.'

As I spoke, tears welled up. *Oh, God.* What was wrong with me? I never got this emotional about schoolwork that was too hard. I'm kind of an average student – I don't shine . . . but I don't worry that much when I struggle either.

So why was not having any control over my visions making me so upset? I looked over at the rose bushes, wiping my eyes.

'Hey.' Nico's voice was tender.

I turned back. He smiled at me.

'I don't think you look stupid,' he said, softly. 'I think you look beautiful.'

For a moment he held my gaze and I felt a great wave of emotion swelling up in my chest. Just like yesterday. My breath caught in my throat and I remembered the promise I'd made yesterday.

'As soon as the bell rings I'm going to find Ed and tell him and everyone we're going out together.'

Nico's smile spread into a huge grin. 'Why don't you try doing a vision again? We've got nearly ten minutes before classes start.'

I closed my eyes, tipped my face to the sun and started my rapid blinking again. This time it was easier to keep the blinking going while I imagined breathing in a deep, sweet scent. Like a gun firing, my heart raced. And then it happened. The flashing lights were there for real . . . the sweet smell truly filling the air.

A jumble of images. Rain. Stone. Ivy. Foster's low menacing voice. 'Kill you, Lex.' The gun, shining wet in the rain. Foster presses the tip against Lex's throat.

I came out of the vision with a gasp. Nico's hand was holding mine. The sun was shining on the rose beds.

'Ketty?' He sounded anxious. 'Ketty? Are you all right?'

I nodded, torn between a desire to smile that I'd brought on a vision at will and concern over what I'd seen.

I described the vision to Nico. '*God*, I wish I knew *when* what I was seeing was going to happen.'

Nico squeezed my hand. 'Don't beat yourself up about it,' he said. 'What you just did was massive. You brought on a vision. That's amazing.'

I smiled. 'Well, it's a start.'

As we left the Tranquillity Garden I kept hold of Nico's hand. For some reason the prospect of telling everyone we were together made me feel really anxious, but I was determined to keep my promise. We sauntered along the narrow path outside the Garden. Someone was sitting, hunched over, on the bench at the end of the path. As we got closer I realised it was Ed.

He was crying.

9: Telling Ed

I glanced at Nico, then stopped. We were less than a metre away from Ed now, but he didn't see us. He was still sitting on the bench outside the Tranquillity Garden, his face in his hands. Tears leaked out on either side as he wept in huge, racking sobs.

I swallowed, feeling uncomfortable. I glanced at Nico again. *What should we do?*

Nico shrugged.

Letting go of his hand, I took a step closer to Ed.

'Hey,' I said, timidly.

Ed's head shot up. He took in both of us in an instant, then started wiping his eyes, furiously. 'Hi,' he said.

'What's the matter?' I asked.

Ed shot a look in Nico's direction. 'Nothing.'

A short pause, then Nico cleared his throat. 'Guess I'll see you inside, Ketts,' he said drily.

I smiled to show I appreciated him letting me talk to Ed without making a fuss. Nico strolled off and I sat down next to Ed.

'Okay,' I said. 'Now tell me.'

Ed stared at his lap. 'It's this whole stupid Medusa thing,' he said. 'Remember Geri called me back to school yesterday, when you went off to the Rufus Stone?'

I blinked. Was that really only yesterday?

'How did it go by the way?' Ed said.

'I'll tell you in a minute,' I said. 'What did Geri want?'

'To test out the parameters of my so-called Gift,' Ed said bitterly. 'She forced me to mind-read her *and* to communicate information.' He sank his head back into his hands. 'I felt like a monkey doing tricks. And all the time Geri was saying stuff like "this is marvellous, dear . . . what a wonderful Gift you have, dear".' Ed curled his lip and looked up, across the grass. 'Patronising cow.'

I stared at him, shocked. I'd never seen Ed so angry and upset.

'It's just so wrong them making us use what we can do, like this.' Ed was sniffing, clearly trying not to cry again. It's bad enough just *having* my ability . . . you know, not being able to look anyone in the eye without getting sucked inside their head . . . but actually *trying* to find out what people are thinking . . . it's horrible . . .'

'It must be awful . . .' I hesitated. 'My visions are a bit like that. I mean, I don't have any control over when they come either . . .'

Ed nodded. 'Mr Fox is the only person who knows how I feel. I can't talk to my parents . . . I called Geri just now to try and explain again and she wouldn't listen . . .' he turned to me, '. . . and *you've* been avoiding me since you went on that stupid mission to the Fostergames offices, so I'm guessing *you* think I'm being ridiculous too.'

'No.' I put my hand on his arm. 'No, I don't think that at all. That's not why I didn't see you . . . I . . . I thought you were with your other friends.' I tailed off lamely.

'What other friends?' Ed wiped his face again. 'I don't *have* any other friends, Ketty. You're the only one.'

There was a silence as the sun went behind a cloud. Two girls from the year above strolled past us, deep in conversation. Inside school, the registration bell rang.

'Sorry.' Ed flushed, straightening up. 'I didn't mean to get all serious with you. It's just . . .'

He let the end of his sentence hang in the air. But I was only too aware of what he meant. Ed and I had gone out, then I'd finished it. And not going out with him was fine . . . but it was important to Ed that I was still in his life.

And, if I was honest, I needed him as a friend too.

'So we're okay?' Ed asked, nervously adjusting his belt. 'Ketty?'

'Of course.' I hugged him and we strolled inside.

As soon as I got to our form room I went over to Nico. He was standing by his desk, sorting some stuff in his bag. Our classmates crowded past. Curtis was showing Lola a picture on his phone. Other people swarmed round them, craning their necks to get a look.

'Nico?'

He didn't look up at me. Just carried on sorting his bag. 'Did you tell him?' he said.

Oh my God.

'I couldn't,' I stammered. 'He was crying. It wasn't the right moment.' Surely Nico would understand that. 'Plus I'm his only friend . . . he *said* so, which made it extra hard for me to say anything. I mean, suppose he'd asked how long you and I had been going out? I couldn't have lied. And if I'd told Ed we'd been together since he and I split up, he'd have felt even worse.'

'Right,' Nico said. 'So you've changed your mind about telling him?'

'Of course not, I just couldn't do it right then.'

At that point, Mr Rogerson walked in and told everyone to sit down. Curtis put his phone away and Lola and the others drifted back to their seats.

Nico shoved his bag under his desk and sat. He stared stonily in front of him.

'I *will* tell Ed about us,' I whispered.

'Right,' Nico said again, his voice like ice. 'Excuse me if I don't hold my breath, babe.'

'Ketty, please take your seat,' Mr Rogerson ordered.

I turned and made my way across the room. I felt sick. Why was Nico being so unreasonable? Okay, so I'd told him I'd tell Ed about us straight away – but he'd *seen* how upset Ed had been outside. *Surely* he couldn't expect me to say something then?

I sat down at my desk, barely aware of Mr Rogerson's

voice droning on as he set us some maths problem. When the bell rang, Nico was first out of the room. We didn't have another class together until after break. I looked for him then, but couldn't find him anywhere.

When break ended I trudged, heavy-hearted, off to English. At least I'd see Nico there. But before I'd got halfway down the corridor Dylan appeared out of nowhere.

I jumped, startled. She grinned, her small white teeth flashing in a perfectly even line. 'Fox's office,' she drawled. 'Now.' She turned and strode away.

I scurried after her. The head's office was just round the corner, but Mr Fox was nowhere to be seen. The others were all in there, though. Geri was talking to Ed by the desk. Nico stood, scowling, on the other side of the room. I gazed at him, hoping he'd look up. But he was pointedly ignoring me.

As Dylan walked in beside me, Geri signalled for her to shut the door.

Geri leaned against the wall, one tan-coloured trouser leg loosely crossed over the other. I opened my mouth to ask her if she'd got the police to find Lex overnight, but before I could say anything she was speaking herself.

'Welcome, team Medusa.' Geri flicked back her hair.

By the desk, Ed shook his head despairingly. Across the room, Nico rolled his eyes. Behind me, Dylan snorted softly under her breath.

I bit my lip. Some team.

Geri cleared her throat. 'Before we get started I should

tell you, Ketty, that there's no news as to your brother's whereabouts yet. But it's still early days.'

I looked down at the floor, my emotions all jumbled up. Where *was* Lex? I felt a stab of resentment towards Nico. Couldn't he see what a hard time I was having? Lex going missing was bad enough, without me having to cope with Nico's ego on top.

'I also want to apologise for the interruption to your training session yesterday. Maria told me what happened and I have had a word with Fergus Fox.'

At this, Nico's head shot up.

Geri glanced at him before she carried on. 'Fergus clearly disagrees with my training strategy, but has accepted that *I'm* in charge of the Medusa Project and promised there will be no further disruptions.'

Nico looked away – I couldn't see his expression.

Ed shook his head again.

'So what's the deal, Geri?' Dylan asked, sprawling across one of Mr Fox's leather chairs. 'I'm missing art for this.'

Geri smiled. 'Thanks to Ketty's lead on Foster,' she said briskly, 'we've found out what Rainbow is.' She paused.

'And . . .?' Dylan asked.

'Rainbow is the nickname for a small, high-explosive device.'

'You mean a *bomb*?' Nico asked.

'Yes – a small but extremely powerful bomb which would cause massive loss of life if detonated in a public area. The MoD has just reported a Rainbow bomb missing. Foster has vanished. His private and company debts are sky-high, so he has a motive for stealing and selling the device. There's no proof, but it all ties up.'

My heart thudded. So Foster had gone through with his plan to steal Rainbow. And Lex's recording was the only evidence that linked him to the crime.

Dylan sat up in her chair. 'What's Foster going to do with the bomb now?'

Geri pursed her lips. 'That, my dear, is what we want the Medusa Project to discover.' She paused. 'In fact, finding out is your next mission.'

10: Accident . . . or murder?

The plan was simple.

Government security agents had already gone into both Foster's home and workplace and searched, secretly, for information about his plans. So far they'd found nothing.

'I don't understand.' Nico made a face. 'If a group of agents couldn't find anything, what d'you expect us to do?'

'Well, it's mostly down to Ketty.' Geri threw me a tight-lipped smile.

'Me?' I said.

'From what Ketty tells us, her brother's most significant contact with Foster occurred in the office car park where he made his recording.' Geri paused. 'I want the four of you to go to the hut by the motorbike stand where Lex overheard Foster talking about Rainbow. My hope is that the setting will prompt Ketty into a vision.'

I shook my head. This was just like when Geri sent me and Nico to the Fostergames office.

I was being used again.

'Why not just take Ketty on her own?' Dylan asked.

'Because I'm trying to build the four of you as a *team*.' Geri stressed the final word.

Dylan rolled her eyes. *She* clearly would have preferred to work alone, or perhaps to do a mission which focused on her own skills – the ability to protect herself from physical harm.

I looked down at my battered old trainers. *I* would have preferred to get my new Asics on, get out of here and go for a proper run.

'Plus,' Geri went on, 'it's an opportunity to be out in the world, ready to use your skills should the need arise.'

'When you say "need",' Ed stammered, 'won't there be security guards in the car park? How are we supposed to get past them?'

'No problem.' Geri smiled her cold, thin-lipped smile. 'Two of my agents – Maria, who you know, and a newer recruit called James – have been briefed to create a distraction, allowing the four of you to slip into the car park undetected. They will also be on hand in case of any problems – but we don't anticipate any. The last place Foster is going to show up is his office. He'll almost certainly suspect by now that we're onto him.'

Ed's shoulders relaxed with relief.

'What am I supposed to do once we're there?' I asked.

The others all stared at me. Dylan was frowning, curled up in her armchair, with her long legs tucked underneath her. I could imagine what she was thinking: *Don't you know how to handle your Gift, Ketty?*

Nico raised his eyebrows. *God*, he was just like Dylan. They both relished their abilities and *wanted* to use them.

I glanced at Ed. He couldn't have looked more miserable. *Like me*, I thought. *Ed is like me. We hate this.*

We hate what we can do.

My heart thudded. Up until now I'd wanted to be more in control of my ability. But now, I realised, I actually didn't want it at all. I didn't want to see visions – or act on them – any more. I just wanted Lex to be safe. And I wanted things to be okay with Nico so that we could hang out and enjoy ourselves like ordinary people.

'I suggest you simply find and explore the hut in the car park, Ketty,' Geri said. 'See what comes up.'

I sat back. Clearly, this was just a shot in the dark for Geri, too.

She talked a little more about our route to central London and where Maria and the other agent were going to drop us off and pick us up.

'Remember, our agents will be in the background at all times. Foster is a dangerous man and Nico and Ketty were lucky to get away without injury when they encountered him.'

'It wasn't luck,' I blurted out. 'It was Nico's telekinesis. He was brilliant.' The words were out of my mouth before I knew I was going to say them. I blushed.

Dylan muffled a giggle. Nico continued to stare at the wall opposite. He idly raised his hand and teleported a box of paper clips off Mr Fox's desk into his palm.

He was acting as if I hadn't spoken.

Geri flicked back her hair impatiently. 'Of course, dear. I meant no disrespect to Nico. I just wanted to make it clear my priority is your protection. You'll leave in ten minutes. Good luck.'

I followed Nico out of the office, determined to make him talk to me.

'Nico?'

He sped up, walking away from me and round the corner.

I stopped. The sick feeling twisted in my guts again. Why was he doing this?

My phone rang. Almost absently I took it out of my pocket and glanced at the screen. I didn't recognise the number.

'Hello?'

'Ketty?' It was Lex. He sounded desperate.

'Where the hell are you? Are you okay?'

'I'm . . .' His voice cracked. 'I'm okay but . . . it's Tessa.'

He stopped. All I could hear was his breathing, fast and shallow. A cold, tight feeling spread across my chest. 'What?' I said. 'Where are you? Where's Tessa?'

Another pause. 'She's dead.' Lex's voice shook as he spoke. 'A car accident on her way to work this morning. Except . . . I'm sure it *wasn't* an accident. Foster must have arranged it . . . killed her. You were right about him, Ketts – somehow he knew I'd made that recording . . . that I gave a copy to Tessa.'

'*Oh God.*' My legs nearly buckled. I couldn't think straight. 'Where are you?'

'Just outside Highgate tube.' Lex paused. 'Ketty, I'm so sorry I didn't listen properly the other day. How did you know—?'

'Never mind about that. Tell me what happened.'

'Okay.' Lex paused, as if collecting his thoughts. 'After I left you, I went after Tessa. I followed her to where she works, but she wouldn't speak to me so I went home and . . .' His voice faltered . . . 'Someone had been there – Foster's men, I guess – searching the place, making a mess. They must have been looking for the recording, though I don't know how they knew I'd even made it—'

'Lex, stop. D'you remember when you left the Rufus Stone? The car coming in the other direction?'

'Vaguely,' Lex said. 'What's that got to—'

'It was Foster. God, Lex, he held me and Nico at gunpoint. We only just got away.'

'*What?*'

'He'd seen you spying on him in the car park and hacked your texts to Tessa.'

'*No*,' Lex said, horrified. 'But that means I put you in danger *and* I led Foster to Tessa. Jesus . . . she's dead because of *me*.'

'No.' *Oh, God.* This was *my* fault. I should have *made* Lex come with me. I should have told Geri about Tessa. She could have protected her.

'Ketty, *please* be careful.' Lex's voice shook with emotion. 'If anything happened to you as well, I couldn't bear it.'

85

'I'll be fine,' I said, trying to push away the guilt about Tessa.

Silence on the end of the phone.

'Lex?'

'How do you know about all this, Ketty? About Foster and the MoD hacking? I . . . I don't understand . . .'

I took a deep breath. 'Okay.' I explained as fast as I could about the Medusa gene and how it was inside the four of us – and how Geri Paterson had forced us to come together as the Medusa Project.

'What?' Lex sounded completely flabbergasted. 'Please tell me you're making this up.'

'I'm not.' I glanced up the corridor. Lola and Billy Martins were walking towards me, hand in hand. I had a bit of a thing with Billy last term. It seemed like a million years ago now. 'Geri knows all about Foster. She was the person who first told me. She's got the police looking for him now. And you.'

'Looking for me?' Lex's voice rose in panic.

'Yes, so she can protect you. You should stay exactly where you are. She can send someone to pick you up.'

Lola and Billy walked past. Neither of them looked at me.

'No.' Lex was almost shouting. 'No. This person you're talking about – Geri Paterson. I don't know why she's telling you you're psychic and involving you in criminal investigations, but it sounds really dodgy. I mean, she's the one who told you about Foster. For all you know it could be her who told Foster about us.'

'What?' I hissed, trying to keep my voice down. 'No, Lex, you've got this all wrong. Geri's head of the Medusa Project, like I told you. In fact she's sending us to Foster's offices right now . . . to that hut in the car park.'

'To Fostergames? Why?'

'To see if searching the place where you made the recording about Rainbow sparks off a vision for me,' I explained. 'Rainbow is a kind of bomb and—'

'A *bomb*? No way, Ketts,' Lex yelled. 'Ketty, you *can't* go to Fostergames, It's ridiculously dangerous. Foster will *kill* you.'

'Calm down,' I said. 'Geri says there's no way Foster will actually be there.'

At the end of the corridor I could see Mr Fox deep in conversation with Ed. Dylan was standing idly next to them, twisting her hair round her finger. She noticed me look up and beckoned me over.

Crap. It was almost time for us to leave.

'Promise me you won't go, Ketts,' Lex pleaded. 'Look, I'll meet you wherever you like. You can take me back with you . . . to this Geri Paterson. But whatever she's told you about psychic powers is rubbish – nobody can see into the future—'

'Yes, they can. *I* can, and—'

'Listen to me,' Lex insisted. 'Even if everything you say is true, then that's all the more reason to stay away from Foster. He's a murderer, and seeing visions of the future won't protect you from that.'

'I know, but he won't be there and anyway the others

have different abilities which *do* protect me. Like Nico . . .
he . . . Anyway . . . Please let me tell Geri – she'll send a car
and—'

'*No*,' Lex said. 'Come yourself. I'll find somewhere more
hidden round here to wait. You can call me when you get to
Highgate.'

'But—'

'It's the only way. Then you'll know I'm safe and I'll
know you're safe.'

I bit my lip. What choice did I have? Lex was in too much
of a state to be reasoned with.

'Okay,' I agreed, reluctantly. 'I'll be there as soon as I can.'

I rang off, changed out of my uniform and into my sweats
and trainers and joined the others at the front door, my mind
reeling. I badly wanted to tell Nico about Lex's call, but he
didn't even look up – he and Dylan were playing a game with
the paper clips Nico had teleported into his hand in Mr Fox's
office. Nico was sending the paper clips zooming through the
air towards Dylan, who was preventing them from hitting her
using her protective force field or whatever it was.

They were laughing as they tried to bat the paper clips
around without anyone seeing. In spite of everything else going
on, I felt a stab of jealousy. They seemed so relaxed together.
Plus Dylan was *so* perfect-looking. That long red hair and
creamy skin and her endless legs in their skinny designer jeans.

Maria and the new agent, James, drove us to Fostergames's
offices.

'Our rendezvous point for the pick-up is the corner of

Parkway, opposite Camden station,' Maria explained. 'We'll be too busy drawing the security guards away from you to pick you up outside the offices – you'll attract less attention if you slip out quietly and make your way on the Northern Line to Camden.'

I sat in the back of the car, chewing on my lip. I wasn't going to be able to get away until they let us out at the Fostergames office. There was no way I could say anything to Nico or Ed without Maria hearing. Anyway, it was better for the others if they didn't know where I was or what I was doing. Whatever happened to me, I didn't want to get anyone else into trouble.

In the end I found the receipt from my Asics in my pocket and scribbled a note to Nico on the back:

I'm really sorry. I know I don't have the right to ask you for any favours but I can't handle this mission. I don't want another vision. I need to be on my own. Please wait for me to call before meeting Maria and James and please stop E and D grassing me up, if you can. Soz for everything. K xxx

We reached the drop-off point. Maria and the other agent stopped to let us out, then sped off towards the Fostergames office.

Dylan sighed and leaned against a nearby wall.

We were supposed to wait until we got a signal from Maria that the coast was clear, then make our way along the final couple of streets to the Fostergames office. I hesitated for a second, then screwed up my note, and shoved it into Nico's hand. Before he had time to react, I'd turned and raced away. I ran as fast as I could, in and out of the crowds on nearby Long Acre.

I stopped, panting, at Leicester Square tube. I looked over my shoulder. No sign of the others.

I took the Northern Line up to Highgate and called Lex as soon as I exited the station. He was in the local cemetery. 'It's massive,' he said. 'Really old with loads of places to hide out. Just walk down the hill and turn right.'

There were several missed calls from Nico on my phone. I ignored them and followed Lex's directions into a park and, from there, to the cemetery. He was right – it was huge. There was even a section you had to pay to visit. I made my way past a large tomb and headed down the overgrown path Lex had directed me to.

I was so intent on reaching him that it was a full ten seconds before I realised my surroundings were somehow familiar. I stopped, my heart racing. And then the sun went behind a cloud and the whole place fell into shadow. Flashing lights raced in front of my eyes. The air grew sweet and still and heavy.

Rain. Leaves. Ivy. Stone. Gun.

A flash of a vision in the corner of my eyes. I blinked it away. Took another step.

Foster's angry eyes fixed on Lex. His gun, wet in the rain. Rain on ivy. Stone.

I shook myself out of the vision. Terror filled my whole body as the realisation hit home.

This was it. This was where my vision took place. I glanced up at the sky. The clouds were dark and threatening. You could smell the rain in the air.

Oh, God, it was about to happen. Everything I'd seen was about to happen.

Foster was here.

Lex was here.

Lex was going to die.

11: The end of the vision

I broke into a run. If Foster was already here, he could be anywhere. I raced down the uneven path. Lex had told me to look out for a large tree set beside a huge gravestone topped with a square, sculpted cross.

As I ran, various possibilities sped through my mind. Maybe Foster was already with Lex ... Oh God, maybe he'd already carried out his threat to kill him ...

I hurtled along. Where was the tree? The gravestone?

Then I saw a large tree up ahead. Beside it was a huge, broken-down stone half hidden by branches and crowned with an elaborate cross. Was that it?

I skidded to a stop. Low voices drifted towards me. I switched my phone to vibrate and crept closer.

There was Lex, standing in front of a tall, ivy-clad gravestone. My stomach lurched as I saw it. *That* was the stone in my vision.

As if on cue, a slow drizzle of rain began to fall. I crept a little closer. I could see Foster now. Calm but menacing – in grey trousers and a crisp, white shirt.

The rain fell harder. It pattered on the stones and leaves around us. This was the scene from my vision. Gravestones covered in ivy and faded writing. Rain streaming down, darkening the stones, dripping down my neck.

'But you killed Tessa . . . she hadn't done *anything* to you.' Lex's voice shook with anger and fear.

'She would have,' Foster said softly. 'After I'd hacked your text to her and followed you to the Rufus Stone I did some investigating. Once I realised she was a journalist it was relatively straightforward to hack into her home computer. She'd managed to find out what the Rainbow was and had emailed her news editor at 2 a.m. with the promise of a "big story in the morning". She told them she had a recording that would implicate a major businessman in a government crime. I had no choice. I had to shut her up. I had to get her copy of your recording.'

'How did you know I was here?' Lex asked. 'I got rid of my old phone.'

'Yes, but you bought a new one under your real name. Once I got the new number I just had to wait for you to make another call – to your sister, Ketty, wasn't it? I triangulated your position half an hour ago and got straight over here.' Foster cleared his throat. 'You're meeting Ketty here, aren't you? I'd like to meet her myself . . . I've got a few questions for her . . .'

I froze behind my tombstone. What the hell did *that* mean?

'I don't know what you're talking about,' Lex snarled. 'Leave my sister out of this.'

93

I held my breath, too overwhelmed for a second to think straight.

'Where is the recording?' Foster pointed his gun at Lex, his eyes cold and angry.

Lex held out his phone. 'On here.'

'This has everything? What I said about the MoD data?' Foster asked, taking the mobile.

'Yes, it's the only copy.'

I shivered, rain trickling down my face. This was *exactly* what I'd seen in my vision.

'What about after you made the recording? Did you look inside the car park hut? Did you see the tile . . . the hiding place? Did you tell anyone?'

'No,' Lex said.

Tile? Hiding place? I scrabbled for my phone.

More calls and angry texts from Nico:

At hut. Where r u?

Told E n D u meetng us here . . . hurry up!!!!

Ed ok but D losing it . . . CALL ME . . .

I quickly sent a text back.

Had vision . . . som sort of hdng plce in hut. A tile? Somthng to do with Rainbow is in there.

94

'Did she . . . Tessa, the car accident . . . was it quick?' Lex's voice shook with emotion.

'Quick enough.' Foster smiled – a mean, cruel smile. 'It looked like an accident – which was the point . . . And it's your own fault. What happened to the girl was inevitable after you gave her that recording.'

'You bastard.' Lex lowered his voice. I could only just hear him over the drumming of the rain. My clothes were completely stuck to me now. Rain plastered Foster's hair to his face. Lex wiped the wetness off his cheek.

'Killing the girl was the only option.' Foster's voice was a low rumble. He turned slightly so I could see right into his furious eyes. 'And now I'm going to have to kill you, Lex.'

No. I forgot the phone in my hand and Nico and the others in the car park.

This was real. This was now. My whole body was shaking.

Do something. DO something.

Foster strode towards Lex, gun outstretched. He pressed the tip against Lex's throat. 'Just tell me one thing – your sister and her boyfriend have some extraordinary powers . . .' Foster paused. 'Does the name Medusa mean anything to you?'

My head spun. How did Foster know about Medusa?

'Leave Ketty alone.'

'I don't think you're in any position to make demands,' Foster said, smoothly. 'Do you?'

Lex stared at him. His heart was beating so fast I could see his chest thumping through the thin shirt, now pasted wet to his skin.

Foster pressed the gun closer to Lex's neck. I looked wildly round, praying for someone . . . anyone . . . to be here. If only Nico was here. If only I'd defied Lex and got Geri to send someone to pick him up.

But it was down to me. At least Foster hadn't seen me.

'Give me your wallet and phone,' Foster demanded. 'This is going to look like a random mugging.'

Hands shaking, Lex reached into his pockets.

This was my chance. Now.

I lunged forwards, knocking Foster sideways. He stumbled, the gun falling from his hand. I snatched it up and held it out.

'Ketty.' Lex was white-faced beside me.

I stared at Foster, the gun outstretched in front of me.

'Put that down.' He reached out for the gun.

'Get back,' I shouted. My hand shook. 'Stay back.'

Foster dropped his hand. His white shirt was soaked, the sleeves clinging to his arms. 'You don't know what you're doing.' He sounded sure of himself, but there was a wary look in his eye. With a jolt I realised he was scared of what I might be able to do, what powers I might have . . .

'We're leaving,' I said. 'Stay here or . . .'

A trickle of rain dripped down my nose. I wiped it away.

'Or *what*?' Foster said, smoothly. 'I'm curious about you, Ketty . . . you and your boyfriend and your other, special, friends . . . there are four of you, aren't there? Viper, Cobra, Sidewinder and Mamba.'

Oh, God. He even knew our Medusa code names.

Foster reached out his hand again. 'Give me the gun and we'll talk and everything will be okay.'

I shook my head. Into the stillness, my phone vibrated. A text. For a split second I jumped, startled. In that tiny moment, Foster lunged forwards, grabbed my wrist and twisted it.

'Oww!' I yelped with pain.

'Get off her!' Lex swung a punch.

Foster ducked, tugging me round so my back was against his chest, my arm twisted behind my back. He took the gun from my hand and pressed it against my ribs.

Lex moved towards us.

'Not another step,' Foster warned. He dug the tip of the gun against my side. The rain was still beating down but I hardly felt it. *He's going to kill me.* My heart raced. For a second I thought I was going to pee myself.

'Mobile,' Foster hissed into my ear.

I held up my phone. Raindrops splashed against the screen. Foster dragged me back into the shelter of the huge tree.

'Show me that text.' He pressed the gun against my ribs.

'Please,' Lex pleaded.

'I've told you already. Stay back.'

Hand shaking, I opened the message. Foster read it over my shoulder.

Found hdng place . . . flash drive inside!!! Taking flash drive n leaving now. Where cn u meet us? I cnt cover 4 u bk @ skool. soz 2 . . . pls call . . . Nxxx

Foster sucked in his breath. 'They're in the car park hut? They've found the flash drive?'

I nodded.

Foster swore. The gun pressed harder against my ribs. 'Is it Medusa doing this?'

I gasped. 'How do you know about Medusa?'

Foster leaned closer, his breath hot in my ear. 'Blake Carson is not a man who makes up stories . . .'

My stomach twisted into a knot. Blake Carson was the man Jack Linden had sold us out to. He was a weapons dealer who'd wanted to buy the Medusa gene formula, then sell it on to criminals around the world. He'd even planned to take Nico with him as proof that the formula worked.

'You know Carson?' I said, my voice trembling.

'I know *of* him – there were some pretty interesting rumours circulating around the time of his arrest a few weeks ago. Something about a group of teenagers with psychic powers working for the government. I didn't think much of it at the time, but after our little run-in at the Rufus Stone, I spoke to a contact of mine inside the security services. He confirmed the rumour was true. You're part of an experiment called the Medusa Project, headed by a government agent called Geri Paterson.'

I stared at Foster, as the rain plastered my hair to my head.

98

'Stop,' Lex insisted. 'Let Ketty go.'

'Out of interest, have all three of your little friends gone to the car park to steal my schematic?' Foster raised his gun, so the cold metal pressed against my neck.

I nodded, shuddering. 'But two agents are following them . . .' I added. 'They're protected.'

Foster narrowed his eyes. 'Do they *all* have telekinetic powers?' he asked.

'Yes . . . no . . . I mean, yes . . .' *Shit. Shit. Shit.* What should I say? What was most likely to keep them safe? I couldn't think straight.

Foster pulled out his phone. 'Soames?' he snapped. 'Where are you?'

Soames said something I couldn't hear.

Foster turned. 'Get to the Fostergames car park. Now. Some kids have found the schematic. Go.' A pause, while Soames presumably said something. 'Watch out for the two agents shadowing them . . . I expect the kids'll be on the street by now,' Foster went on. 'There's a boy. About fifteen. Dark hair and eyes.' He paused again, pressing the gun harder against my neck. 'Describe the others.'

I wanted to lie but my mind couldn't work out what to say. 'Er . . . a girl with long legs and long red hair. She's in jeans. And, er . . . another boy. Tall with sandy hair. He's wearing chinos.' *Oh, God . . . oh, God . . .*

Foster repeated my description. 'Where will the two agents be?' he demanded.

'I don't know . . .' I looked away. According to the plan,

Maria and the other agent were going to move away from the area as soon as they'd successfully distracted the car park security officers. If Nico and the others had left the car park, Maria would also be on her way – to the rendezvous point in Camden. I looked back at Foster.

He was studying me carefully, his keen grey eyes piercing me through.

'Soames, your priority is to retrieve the flash drive containing the schematic without being spotted by the two agents shadowing the kids.' He pressed his phone to loudspeaker. 'Soames, do you copy?'

'Yes, sir.' I recognised Soames's voice instantly. He was definitely the man Foster had been talking to in Lex's recording. 'What do you want me to do when I see them?'

I held my breath.

Foster turned to me. 'What can they do to him?' he said. 'What powers do they have?'

'Nothing,' I stammered, not wanting to give the others away. 'I don't know.'

Foster swore.

'Tell him, Ketty,' Lex pleaded.

'Listen to your brother.' Foster cocked his gun and pointed it at Lex. 'Or watch him die.'

Shit. 'Telekinesis, mind-reading, and defence shield,' I said quickly.

Foster considered this for a second, then turned back to his phone.

'Shoot the little bastards on sight.'

100

12: The hostage

'*No.*' My whole body was shaking now. This couldn't really be happening. '*Please*, don't do this. *Please.*'

I was still holding my mobile in my hand. I stood, rigid. There must be some way of stopping Foster. I twisted round a little, so I could see his face. His eyes were hard and grey, like tiny pebbles.

'Please,' I said again. 'I'll do anything you want. Just don't kill them.'

Foster stared at me for a second. Then his eyes flickered back to the text on my phone.

Lex was still standing in the rain, shivering . . . watching . . .

'This "N" your text's from,' Foster said. 'Is that Nico? Is that your boyfriend? The one I met at the Rufus Stone?'

'Yes,' I sobbed. 'Please don't hurt him.'

Foster considered the text again. 'When he says "*soz 2*", what's he sorry about?' he asked.

'Nothing,' I said. Why was Foster asking that? 'Nothing – just a stupid row.'

Foster hesitated a second. Then he raised his phone to his mouth again. 'Soames?'

'Yes, sir,' came the muffled reply.

'Change of plan,' he said. 'Can you see the kids?'

'Yeah,' Soames said. 'They're just outside Fostergames, like you said.'

'Where are they going?' Foster demanded. The cold metal of his gun pressed against my neck.

'Leicester Square tube,' I said, my heart pounding.

'Did you hear that, Soames?' Foster said.

'Yes, sir. I need to move fast. They'll be in a crowded area in less than a minute.'

'Hold fire.' Foster pointed with his gun to my phone. 'Call him. And put your phone on speaker.'

I stared at him. 'Call who?'

'Your boyfriend. "*Nico*". Tell him you're sorry about whatever it is too and that all three of them are to wait for you at Leicester Square station. You'll meet them there.'

'Why?'

'I'll explain in a minute.'

'No.' My voice rose. I couldn't put the others in any more danger. '*No.*'

'You've got three seconds to dial, or I'm ordering Soames to shoot. Three.'

'Wait.' I lifted my mobile. Hesitated.

'Two.'

'Okay, I'll do it.' Hands shaking, I put my mobile on loudspeaker and dialled Nico.

'Remember, make sure all three of them wait for you,' Foster cautioned.

Nico's phone rang. 'Babe?' he said. 'What the hell are you doing?'

'I'm so, so sorry I didn't tell Ed after I'd promised I would . . .' I stopped, tears threatening to choke my voice.

'Sssh. Where are you? Are you all right?' Nico lowered his voice. 'I'm sorry too, I was an arsehole earlier. I know Ed was upset. It's just you promised—'

'I know,' I cut in, my eyes on Foster. He moved forwards a step and pressed his gun against Lex's temple. 'I'm *really* sorry, Nico.'

I could hear Dylan's voice in the background. 'We need to go.'

'Your vision worked, though, Ketts,' Nico went on. 'We went over the whole hut. Found the loose tile . . . Are you really all right?'

'Course, I just needed to be on my own for a bit. I'm sorry I bailed on you earlier.'

'It doesn't matter. It all worked out in the end, didn't it?' He hesitated. 'I really want to see you.'

'Me too,' I said. Foster was still staring at me, his eyes mean and hard, his gun still pressed against the side of Lex's head. 'I'm coming back. I don't want to get into trouble. Wait for me at Leicester Square, yeah?'

'Okay, but—'

'All of you, Nico. Please, it's important. I need to be sure you'll all cover for me.'

'Course we will. Well, me and Ed will def—'

'Make Dylan wait too.' I swallowed. 'She'll do it if *you* ask.'

'Okay.' Nico sounded uncertain. 'Babe, are you sure everything's all right. You sound weird.'

'Yeah, I'm fine.' I hesitated. 'I just had some thinking to do. See you in a bit.'

I told Nico where to wait for me at Leicester Square then rang off and turned to Foster. 'I don't understand,' I said. 'What's this about?'

A thin smile curled round Foster's lips. He raised his phone again. 'Soames, change of plan. Don't approach the kids. Let them go.'

I waited. The rain stopped. Foster lowered his gun. He looked from me to Lex.

'Don't hurt Ketty,' Lex pleaded.

I pushed my soaking hair off my face. 'What do you want me to do?'

'I want you to erase the contents of the flash drive your friends have just found,' Foster said.

'*What?*' I frowned. 'How am I supposed to do that? Geri'll pounce on us as soon as we're back, demanding a debrief.'

'Is Lex your only brother?' Foster asked.

'Yes.'

'I have a brother, too,' Foster said. 'Rick. It's a special bond.'

I frowned. Foster had mentioned a brother before. 'What's having a brother got to do with this?' I asked.

'Rick's in jail for a crime he didn't commit,' Foster said. 'I've spent the past year paying lawyers to build an appeal which hasn't worked. Hundreds of thousands of pounds . . . me and my company up to our eyes in debt . . . for nothing.'

I stared at him, remembering what Geri had told us earlier. 'So that's why you need the Rainbow bomb,' I said. 'You're going to sell it so you can pay off your debts.'

'What I'm planning to do with the Rainbow is none of your business,' Foster went on. 'All you need to worry about is deleting what's on that flash drive.'

'How?' I said.

'If your brother means as much to you as mine does to me, you'll find a way,' Foster said, softly. 'Remember, I don't want the stick itself destroyed, just the contents got rid of.'

'What if I refuse?' I said, my throat tightening. I was suddenly aware of how cold I was – my clothes clinging to me, damp against my skin.

'You won't,' Foster said, smoothly. 'And you won't go behind my back to anyone, either. As I told you before, I've got a source in the government security agency, close to Geri Paterson, so I'll know straight away if you tell her what I'm really planning.'

Foster paused, shifting his gaze to Lex. 'It's simple. If Geri Paterson finds out, then I'll kill your brother – and come after the four of you.'

13: The schematic

I don't know how I made it back to Leicester Square. I was too shocked to think straight, acting on autopilot. Foster was holding my brother hostage – and if I didn't do what he demanded, Lex would die.

But how on earth was I going to get the flash drive the others had found – and delete the information that was on it?

I fought my way down the escalators at the tube station. There was some delay on the Northern Line so the platform where I was meeting the others was packed. I looked round but I couldn't see them.

And then Nico appeared, weaving his way through the crowd towards me.

He stopped just in front of me.

'I'm sorry.'

'I'm sorry.'

We both spoke at once. Then Nico hugged me. It was so good to feel his arms round me. For a second I almost told him what Foster had asked me to do. But I couldn't. Suppose he insisted on telling Geri? After all, Foster was planning to sell a bomb which had the potential to kill thousands of people. If Nico spoke to Geri, Foster said his source would know straight away. And if the source told Foster, then Lex would be dead before anyone could attempt to rescue him.

Guilt threaded its way through my head. Could I really put my brother's life ahead of saving others? It was an impossible choice.

'Man, I felt so bad when you got off the train earlier,' Nico said. 'And when I read your note I felt even worse. I'm . . . er, Ed's got the flash drive . . . I'm sorry I was such an arse about him earlier.'

'Me too,' I said, pulling back from the hug. At some point I was going to have to sort everything between me and Nico and Ed out, but right now all I could think about was saving Lex.

Nico smiled at me, but his eyes were anxious. 'Are you really okay? You're all wet.'

I took a deep breath. 'I'm fine, I've just been walking around. Come on, lets get back to the others.'

Together we walked back through the commuter crowds. Ed glanced up at me, half smiling, though not properly meeting my eyes as usual.

Dylan raised her eyebrows, all mock shocked. '*Oh. My. God*,' she said with exaggerated emphasis. 'It's the Grunge Princess . . . *oooh*, we're *sooo* honoured you've decided to turn up at last . . .'

'Piss off.' I was in no mood to deal with her attitude.

'What did you say?' Dylan's mouth set in a grim line. She drew herself up. 'Come here and say that again.'

I gritted my teeth. *God*, she was a whole head taller than me. If she hit me I wouldn't stand a chance. On the other hand, she'd been asking for a punch in the mouth ever since I'd met her. More people were crowding on the platform but I was only dimly aware of them. I clenched my fists, all my fear and frustration focused on Dylan's green eyes.

'I said you're a rude cow. What you gonna do about it?'

Dylan stared at me. She hadn't moved a muscle, but I could see a flicker of fear in her eyes.

'Ketty,' Ed gasped.

'If you two are going to fight,' Nico grinned, 'you'd make it a lot more fun for the rest of us if you'd just take your tops off.'

'Shut up, Nico.' I turned to Dylan. 'Go on then, try and hit me.' I raised my fists. 'Just try.'

Dylan hesitated for a second, then stuck her nose in the air and stalked off. Yanking her mp3 player out of her pocket, she disappeared behind a knot of tourists jostling round a tube map.

A train rumbled into the station.

'Wow,' Nico said, a note of admiration in his voice. 'You really *were* pissed off.' I smiled at him, feeling better than before. We got on the tube. It was as crowded as the platform – just three seats available in the whole carriage. A couple of doors down Dylan was getting on. She took the seat furthest away from us, turning heads as she sashayed towards it in her jeans and cropped jumper. Ed sat down at the end of the nearest row. The only other vacant space was opposite him.

'D'you wanna sit down?' Nico asked, gruffly.

I nodded gratefully and scooted into the seat. The tube train set off. I glanced at the station list above the seats and my sense of feeling better drained away. In just six stops we'd be at Camden – where Maria would be waiting for us, demanding to see the flash drive the others had found . . .

My palms were clammy with sweat and my top still felt damp against my skin. I glanced along the carriage. Nico was standing a few metres away in the gap between the seat sections, bent over his phone. Dylan had jammed in her headphones and was listening to music. Loud music. Even from here I could hear its insistent beat thudding round the carriage.

I looked over at Ed opposite. He had his nose deep in some book. I leaned forwards and tapped him on the knee.

His head jerked up, reddening as he almost caught my eye.

'How did it go in the hut in Foster's car park?' I said.

'Fine, I guess,' Ed muttered. 'Nico got us in past the lock on the door, while Dylan made snotty remarks about everything.'

'About *me*?'

'About *everything*,' Ed said firmly. 'I asked Nico where you were. He kept insisting you'd catch up with us. Then you sent that text about the tile.'

'Yeah.' I hesitated. 'So what . . . where . . . what did you find? Was the tile the hiding place?'

'Yeah, a loose ceiling tile . . . we found a USB flash drive taped underneath it.' Ed blushed. 'I found it, actually. Not that it was hard to find – the only tiles in the hut were in the ceiling. I mean you couldn't tell from looking that they were loose but we poked them until one came free.'

'Can I have a look at it?'

'Er . . . sure . . .' Ed rummaged in his pocket. 'Er . . . why?'

'I thought maybe holding it would spark off another vision . . .'

'Here.' Ed handed me the little stick.

Now what was I supposed to do? Maybe I could destroy it – drop the wretched thing as we got off the train – or let it slip onto the tracks in the gap between the tube train and the platform.

No. Foster had stressed I was to delete what was on the flash drive, not destroy it. If I wanted to make sure Lex would be safe, that's what I had to do. I fingered the flash drive. Lex's terrified face flashed into my head. Where was Foster going to take him now? Would he hurt him?

Oh, God.

'Ketty, are you okay?' Ed's kindly blue eyes were full of concern.

I glanced at his bag. Suddenly I had an idea. 'Sure.' I held up the flash drive. 'But this thing isn't prompting anything except a headache.' I leaned forward and pretended to drop it inside his bag. As I did so I gripped the edge of his laptop,

110

poking out at the top. 'Can I borrow this for a sec? I just remembered a bit of homework I was supposed to do. If I don't write it down now I'll forget again.'

'Okay.'

I tugged the laptop out, hiding the flash drive in my palm. I sat back and opened up the computer. I created a word document and quickly wrote down the title of an English essay we were supposed to be writing, then some random page numbers.

I looked up. Nico was still busy with his phone and Ed had gone back to his book. Dylan had her eyes shut and was nodding her head in time to the music on her mp3 player. If anything it was even louder than before.

I went back to the computer and closed my word doc. One of Ed's folders caught my eye – *Rainbow Bomb Research*. In spite of the stress of the situation I couldn't help smiling. Ed even did homework for Medusa missions.

The man sitting next to me was reading a newspaper. As quietly as I could, I felt my way to the USB port on the side of the laptop and plugged the flash drive in. I glanced down the carriage. Nobody was looking at me. I positioned the laptop so the little stick was turned away from Ed and hidden from Nico and Dylan by my neighbour's paper.

My heart pounded as I opened the file inside. A set of blueprints . . . the layout of a building. This must be what Foster had referred to as a 'schematic'. My eyes flickered to the name of the building: Gayton General Hospital in South London.

What did a hospital have to do with Foster's plan to sell the bomb? I closed the file then glanced sideways. Ed was still deep in his book.

I highlighted the file and pressed 'delete'. The computer asked me if I was sure.

Yes. How could I do anything else? This was the only way.

A second later the whole flash drive was wiped clean.

I quickly yanked it out of the laptop and, leaning forward again, shoved both laptop and flash drive back into Ed's bag.

He glanced up at me and half-smiled. I sat back, my hands shaking.

Oh God, what had I done?

14: The plant

A few minutes later we reached Euston. Half the carriage emptied, so Nico was able to sit down next to me. He asked if I'd heard from Lex. I said I had – and that Lex had managed to get away from Foster and was staying with some friends who lived in France.

I hated lying to him but I just couldn't see an alternative. I changed the subject as quickly as possible, asking Nico how he'd got past the lock on the hut in Foster's car park. He shrugged ... said it was easy ... but I could tell he was pleased that I'd asked.

We chatted a bit. It should have made me feel great that everything was okay between us but all I could do was worry. Would I be responsible for what Foster did with the Rainbow bomb? What was Geri going to say when we arrived back at school empty-handed? Was Lex okay?

A car met us at the station. Dylan was still, pointedly, listening to music through her headphones. The bass pounded through the car as we drove back to school. Dylan made no attempt to talk to any of us. She didn't even take the head-phones off until we arrived back at school. I didn't care any more. Dylan's rudeness was the last thing on my mind – I'd lost all appetite for a fight now that we were so close to home.

Geri was at the school gates, smartly dressed as always in beige trousers and a pale pink twin set. As she led us to Mr Fox's office, I told her Lex was in France.

'That explains why the police haven't picked him up, then.' She adjusted the pearls round her neck. 'Is he safe?'

I hesitated for a second, almost unbearably tempted to tell her what was really going on. Then I remembered what Foster had said about having a source inside the government security agency. I couldn't afford to risk telling Geri the truth. If Foster found out I'd betrayed him, he'd kill Lex for sure.

'Yes, Lex is fine.' The lie cut me like a knife. 'I don't know where he is in France though.'

'I'll get Interpol onto it straight away. We need him back with that recording asap.'

I nodded, feeling numb.

Mr Fox was waiting for us by his office door, all solemn and concerned. 'I've told Geri that you have to make up the lessons you've missed today,' he said.

'What?' Nico screwed up his face, annoyed. 'What kind of a thank you is that?'

'Room 14, when the school day finishes,' Mr Fox went on, ignoring him. 'I've asked all your teachers to provide me with the work you've missed. I'm going to personally over-see your assignments.'

'Excellent,' Nico muttered. 'I can't wait.'

Geri swept past us, into the office. Mr Fox stared, sullenly, after her, but didn't protest as Geri called the four of us inside and shut the door in his face.

'Right, now let's see what you've got.' Geri held out her hand and Ed passed her the USB flash drive.

She inserted it into Mr Fox's PC. Everyone else crowded round but I hung back on the edge of the group, my heart pounding.

A blank screen appeared. 'What is this?' Geri's voice rose. 'Where are the contents?'

All eyes turned on Ed. *Oh, God.*

'I don't know,' he stammered. 'It's just been in my bag . . .'

'What a loser,' Dylan snarled. 'All that effort for nothing.'

Geri's lips were pursed tightly together. 'Damn,' she said.

'Why would Foster go to the trouble of hiding an empty flash drive?' Nico said.

'It doesn't make sense,' Geri agreed. She looked at me.

'My vision just showed a loose tile in the hut,' I lied, 'it was only a hunch that Foster might have hidden something in it.'

'Maybe Foster was waiting for data to be put *onto* the flash drive,' Dylan suggested.

'That's possible I suppose.' Geri shot a suspicious look at Ed.

His face was burning red. Guilt flooded through me.

Geri asked some more questions about the mission. I made up a few details about my supposed vision, then shut up and let Nico and Dylan explain how they found the flash drive. Nobody mentioned my absence at the car park.

After about twenty minutes, Geri set off for central London in her car. I left Nico, still grumbling about having to do an extra class after school finished, and went for a run. It was the end of lunch break so I didn't have much time but I had to get away from everyone. I ran and ran, letting my head clear. I ran right through the two playing fields to the edge of the school grounds, then back round the Top Field. At last I stopped, exhausted. I was going to be late for afternoon lessons, but I didn't care.

Just then my phone rang. *Number withheld.*

'Hello?' I said, anxiously.

'Ketty?' It was Foster.

'Is Lex okay?' I said. 'Have you let him go?'

'Lex is fine. More importantly, my source tells me the flash drive arrived empty.' He cleared his throat. 'I'm assuming you had a look before deleting it. Did you understand what you saw?'

I thought rapidly back to the contents of the memory stick.

'It was a hospital,' I said. 'And, no, I didn't understand. What's a hospital got to do with you selling a bomb?'

There was silence on the other end of the phone. And, in that moment, I suddenly realized that Foster had never intended to *sell* the Rainbow bomb. His plan was to *use* it himself.

116

'You're going to blow up the hospital, aren't you?' I blurted out. 'You're going to hurt loads of innocent people – for absolutely no reason.'

There was a pause and when Foster spoke, his voice was icy. 'I have a reason,' he said.

'So where's Lex?' I asked. 'Let me speak to him.'

Silence. I could hear the phone being passed between hands.

'Ketty are you okay?' Lex was talking fast . . . breathless . . . 'I'm being held in an empty building near—'

'That's enough.' Foster was back.

'I did what you asked,' I said. 'Now let him go.'

'I don't think I'm ready to do that quite yet.'

Foster's calm, menacing voice slid through me like ice water.

'What d'you mean?' I stammered.

'Just that there's something else I want you to do for me first. After school I want you to call Geri Paterson and tell her you've had a "vision".'

'A vision?' I said. 'Of what?'

'Me on the phone explaining that I'm about to plant the Rainbow bomb at Linhurst Hospital, in East London.'

'*Linhurst* Hospital?' I repeated the name, my head spinning. Linhurst wasn't the name of the hospital whose blueprints were on the flash drive. That was *Gayton* Hospital in *South* London.

'Tell Ms Paterson that you've seen me on the phone saying I'm at Linhurst and that I'm about to plant the Rainbow bomb somewhere in the hospital.'

Oh God, oh God . . . 'My . . . my visions are usually more hazy than that . . .' I said, playing for some time to think.

'That's no problem,' Foster said quickly. 'In fact, I *want* you to be hazy about the bomb's exact location inside the hospital. That way the police will be kept busy searching for me—'

'. . . while you set off the actual bomb somewhere else.' *Of course.* That explained why the schematic I'd seen on that USB drive was of a different hospital.

Foster sucked in his breath. 'You do realise your brother's life depends on you keeping my actual intentions quiet.'

I gasped at the enormity of the lie I would have to tell. 'You're asking me to give the police fake data and stand by while you explode a bomb in *another* hospital?'

'Yes. The one thing you must be specific about is when the bomb is going to go off,' Foster went on. 'Timing is everything here. Tell them you heard me saying it's set to detonate first thing tomorrow morning – 6 a.m.' He paused. 'Do you understand?'

'Yes,' I said. 'Rainbow bomb. Linhurst Hospital. 6 a.m. tomorrow.'

'Good.' He rang off.

I stood, the phone in my hands and the wind on my face. It felt like the world was whirling around me.

I trudged back towards the school complex trying to get my head around what I had to do: pretend to have a vision and give Geri Paterson false information.

I stopped in my tracks as the full weight of the situation hit me.

This could carry on forever.

As long as Foster had Lex, he had me in his power – he could get me to do whatever he wanted.

I went back to my dorm, changed and then walked in a daze to my next lesson. I don't remember what subject it was. I looked round me – at Tom and Lola flirting with each other . . . at Curtis copying someone's homework under his desk.

I'd been like them once . . . living just for my running, my biggest worry whether I'd ever get to run a marathon . . .

I stayed in a daze for the rest of the afternoon.

Could I really do what Foster asked? Destroying existing evidence was one thing . . . but telling such an enormous lie was *evil*. A hospital was going to be blown up – people's lives were at stake.

It was horrible. I couldn't do it.

Except that I knew I had to . . . or else Lex would die.

As soon as school was over for the day, Mr Fox whisked Nico, Ed, Dylan and me off for our extra two-hour session. He told us to give the usual Medusa Project cover story – that the four of us were being given extra maths coaching.

As Nico pointed out before, anyone thinking about it would have realised the strangeness of this in an instant. Ed already got consistently high marks in maths (and everything else), while Nico and I were in a different maths set from Dylan, whose own knowledge on the subject was based on an alternative, thanks to her years at American schools.

I didn't care about any of that today. I just sat there while Nico and Dylan moaned loudly about having to catch up on their classwork and Ed got on with it.

I couldn't see a way out.

If I refused to give Geri the false information, Foster would kill Lex. If I went along with Foster's demands many more people would die when the Rainbow bomb went off.

Finally the two hours were up. I couldn't delay any longer. I had no idea where Geri either lived or worked, but she'd given us an emergency mobile number during our first ever briefing. Heavy-hearted, I headed outside to call her. Nico caught up with me as I passed the main stairs.

'Where are you going?' he demanded.

'I—'

'Doesn't matter.' He grinned. 'You're not going there now, anyway.'

'No?'

'No. You, me, Tom and Lola are going to see a movie.' Nico put his hands on my shoulders. 'Come on. It's what we need . . . getting out of here for a bit. I've got us passes 'til ten.'

I hesitated. There was nothing I'd have liked more than to put Foster and his blackmail out of my head for a couple of hours and escape with my gorgeous boyfriend to the movies, but I *had* to call Geri.

'I can't,' I said.

The smile faded from Nico's face. 'Why?' he said.

I blinked, trying to think up an excuse to be on my own for a while.

'I need to go for a run,' I stammered.

Nico stared at me. 'You'd rather go for a run than hang out with me?' he said slowly. 'After everything that happened today – all the covering up I did for you?'

'It's not like that,' I said.

'What *is* it like, then?' Nico paused, his forehead creased with a frown.

'I just want to be outside,' I repeated, lamely.

'Okay.' Nico shrugged. 'We can hang out in the Top Field.' He reached for his phone. 'I'll text Tom and Lola. Cancel.'

There was nothing I could do. I let Nico send his text, then lead me outside, to the tree where we often met up.

'Mmm,' he said, leaning against the trunk and putting his arms round me. 'So what was all that about earlier? You running off at the car park?'

I shook my head. 'Let's not talk about it,' I said.

Nico grinned. 'Not talking's cool.' He leaned forward and kissed me.

And then my phone rang.

'Don't answer,' Nico said, lowering his mouth to my neck.

I pulled out my mobile and glanced at the screen over his shoulder.

Number withheld

Shit. It had to be Foster. The phone rang again. I hesitated.

'Switch it off,' Nico murmured.

Shit, shit, shit.

121

I disentangled myself. 'It's Lex,' I lied. 'I have to speak to him. Let him know Geri's looking for him . . . that she'll protect him when he comes back to England.

'Go on, then.' Nico sighed, letting me go. 'But don't get into a long one, okay?'

'Okay.'

Nico wandered over to a nearby flower bed and sat on the grass. My phone was still ringing.

I turned away and whispered into it. 'Hello?'

'Problem, Ketty?' Foster's voice was icy. 'My source tells me you've been free from your two-hour, after-school catch-up session for over fifteen minutes and you don't appear to have called Geri Paterson yet.'

I gasped. How did Foster know so precisely what I'd been doing?

'Who told you that?'

'I told you already – my source in the security services,' Foster paused. 'So, what are you waiting for?'

'Nothing.' I glanced over my shoulder. Nico had pulled a handful of coins out of his pocket and was concentrating hard on teleporting them in a circle, just above the grass. The dying sun above our heads glinted off the coins, giving the whole scene a sinister glow.

'You're not making any sense,' Foster said, the threat in his voice unmistakable. 'Which is very bad news for your brother.'

'How do I know you'll even let Lex go once I've done what you ask?'

'When I've got what I want, I won't need him any more,' Foster snapped.

'Why are you setting off a bomb, anyway?' My breath caught in my throat. 'Why do you want to hurt a load of innocent people?'

There was a long pause. Nico let out an exasperated sigh as one of the coins he was teleporting whizzed off into the bushes.

'I don't want to hurt people.' Foster's voice was suddenly heavy. 'But you'll remember I have a brother too. Rick. It's *all* about Rick. Now go and do what I bloody told you to.'

He rang off.

What did *that* mean? I bit my lip. In the end, it didn't matter what Foster's motives were. I *had* to do what he said. It was Lex's only chance.

I wandered uneasily back to Nico. He held out his hands and all the coins he was teleporting zoomed into his cupped palms. He shoved them into his pocket and turned to me with a grin.

'Lex okay?'

I nodded, forcing a smile.

'Good.' Nico put his arms round me. 'Now, where were we?'

We kissed for a bit, but Foster's demand kept going through my head.

'Ketty?' Nico pulled away from me. He frowned. 'What's up?'

I hesitated. I *so* wanted to tell him. But it wasn't fair. If he told Geri what I was planning, Lex would die. And if Nico went along with my lie then I'd end up making him responsible for the deaths of all the people in the hospital too.

'Nothing.' I took his face in my hands and tried to kiss him again, but it was no good. I wasn't going to be able to focus on anything else until I'd pretended to have the fake vision Foster wanted. I hesitated for a second. Either I did that now, or I told Nico I didn't feel very well and went inside alone.

Get it over with. All of a sudden I went rigid in his arms. Not breathing . . . my eyes wide and glazed over.

'Ketts?' Nico stood back, staring at me. 'Ketty?'

I stood there, trying not to blink. How long did my visions usually last? From what the others had told me only a few seconds. I counted to five in my head. Nico's breathing was shallow and fast. 'Ketty?' he whispered. He sounded scared.

I hate myself. Four . . . five . . .

I blinked rapidly, letting my body relax. 'Oh . . .' I said. 'Oh my God . . .'

'What was it?' Nico put his arms round me again. 'Was it a vision?'

'Yes,' I said. I told him what Foster had told me to say – that I'd seen him talking . . . saying a bomb was going off at 6 a.m. tomorrow morning in Linhurst Hospital in East London. 'Oh, God, Nico . . . a hospital . . . all those people . . .'

'But you've got a date and a time,' he said. 'Which means

the police'll be able to stop the bomb going off. Geri can send in a team of disposal experts or something.' He tugged me away from our tree, back towards the school. 'Come on, he urged. 'This is big. We should tell her now.'

'Sure.'

Feeling sick to my stomach, I let him take my hand and lead me towards the main school building.

15: The hospital

Everything was in motion now – though Nico, Ed, Dylan and I were no longer part of it. At first, when I told Geri about my 'vision' she sounded a little sceptical – but the fact that I could give her a specific name for the Rainbow bomb's location – Linhurst Hospital – helped convince her. Within a few minutes she was on the phone to some bomb disposal unit, pretending she'd intercepted an email about Foster's intentions, and the hospital was being evacuated. Some of the patients there were very sick but there was, thank goodness, nobody whose life was put in danger specifically by being moved.

Nico found Dylan and told her what was going on. Ed joined them soon afterwards, having spoken to Mr Fox. We stayed up until past midnight, when Mr Fox insisted we all went to bed.

'There's nothing more you can do . . . the officials have everything under control now.'

No, they don't, I wanted to scream. *No, they don't.*

But I kept my mouth shut, even though the guilt I felt was so overwhelming it was like I was drowning in it.

I thought about calling Mum and Dad and telling them Lex was being held hostage. I almost did it, in fact. I mean, it wasn't like we had any kind of normal family life: we only spoke once a week, when Mum called from Singapore. Now we were older we didn't even always fly out to see them during the school holidays, but they still had a right to know what was happening to their own son.

But I couldn't bear to tell them. They'd be straight onto the school which would mean Geri finding out that I'd lied to her. All of which would, simply, put Lex's life in jeopardy.

I tossed and turned, unable to sleep, my little Lex troll doll clutched in my hand. Across the dorm, Lola and Lauren were snuggled up under their respective covers. Dylan was asleep too, breathing heavily with her long hair spread out across the duvet like a red shawl.

My mind darted around. Was Lex okay?

What about everyone at Gayton Hospital, in South London, where the Rainbow bomb was *really* going to go off at 6 a.m.?

I'd lied to Nico. I'd tricked Geri.

Maybe if I focused hard, I could see what was going to happen. Reassure myself no one would actually get hurt. I turned my face to the moonlight and blinked, willing a vision to me . . .

Sweet, heavy perfume filled the air . . . flashing lights . . .

I'm running . . . an endless series of dark corridors . . .
I can't see where I am . . . just running and running . . .
there's someone beside me . . . but I don't look round . . .
I can't see who . . .

I snapped out of the vision. Before I knew what I was doing I was out of bed, heart racing, staring wildly round the dorm. The other girls were still asleep. Dylan had rolled over and was lying on her back, gently snoring. The wardrobe that stood along one wall cast a dark shadow into the room.

I took a deep breath. Everything was where it always was. Everything was as it always was.

Except at Gayton Hospital. I checked the time on my phone. Three a.m. The Rainbow bomb was going off in three hours. My visions clearly weren't going to help save anyone. Even if the dark corridors I'd just seen myself in were in some way relevant, I had no idea where they were – or when I was going to be running through them.

It was suddenly clear to me that I had to call the hospital . . . tell someone I'd seen a man with a bomb, then ring off before anyone asked me any questions.

Foster would never know it was me. Lex would be safe.

Except . . . I'd have to explain how I *knew* it was a bomb. I mean, no one would believe me unless the description I gave matched up with the description of a Rainbow bomb. And I had no idea what a Rainbow bomb looked like.

How could I find out?

The answer came immediately.

Ed. Hadn't I seen a folder called *Rainbow Bomb Research* on his laptop? He must have got the information from the internet. I could log onto one of the school's library computers and do the same thing.

No. That would take too long. I had to see Ed's own file. If I could sneak a look at what *he'd* found then I'd surely have enough information on the bomb to sound convincing.

I hurried into my sweats and trainers and set off for the boys' dormitories. It was totally illegal to venture into their rooms at night, but I didn't care.

I tiptoed along the main hall, down the corridor. Past the canteen and the kitchens and Mr Fox's office, and up the stairs to the boys' dorm that Ed shared with Nico and two other boys. Their door was closed. I opened it as softly as I could and crept inside. The beds were arranged just like in my own dorm. Two beds on one side of the room and two on the other. Nico was in the bed furthest from the door. He was sleeping on his side, his hair across his face. He looked peaceful. Beautiful. My heart twisted as I remembered how I'd lied to him about my vision before.

Ed slept in the bed opposite. As I glanced over he was struggling onto his elbows. 'Ketty?' he whispered. 'Is that you?'

'Ssssh.' I crept a little closer. 'I'm really sorry to wake you. Um, can I borrow your laptop?'

'It's okay, I wasn't asleep.' Ed frowned as he sat up properly. 'Just give me a sec.'

I waited outside. Half a minute later Ed appeared. He was dressed, as usual, in smart chinos and a jumper though his sandy hair was tousled, even for him. His laptop was under his arm.

I held out my hand. 'I just need to borrow it.'

'Er . . . let's go down to the music room in the basement,' he whispered.

'But—'

'Come on, it's soundproofed. We can talk properly there.' Ed headed for the stairs. I had no choice but to follow.

We crept downstairs on tiptoe. The basement was dark and cold. Ed led me past a couple of storage rooms and into the music room. As soon as we were inside he shut the door.

'So, what's this about, Ketty?'

'Nothing much.' I tried to sound casual. 'I was just looking for some information on your laptop . . .'

'And you had to look for it in the middle of the night?'

Shit.

I perched on the piano stool in the corner of the room. It was no good – I couldn't lie any longer. Especially not to Ed.

Anyway, if I was honest, it would be a relief to tell someone.

'Okay, it's the Rainbow bomb,' I blurted out. 'I saw you had a research file on it when I borrowed your laptop the other day. I . . . er, was interested.'

'Right.' Ed rubbed his forehead. 'Why?'

I stared at him. *Oh God.*

'I need to know what it looks like.'

'Oh.' Ed frowned. 'I don't know exactly what it looks like,' he said slowly. 'I mean, I don't have a picture. It's classified information – MoD top secret sort of thing . . .'

I bit my lip. *Of course.* Why hadn't I thought of that? No way were pictures of a high-explosive, state-of-the-art bomb going to be found lying about on easily accessible websites. How stupid was I?

I sank back against the piano. So much for my big idea. It was hopeless. It was *totally* hopeless. Foster was going to set off the Rainbow bomb and innocent people would die and I had no guarantee, even after all of that, that Lex would actually be okay.

I cried – soft, warm tears leaked through my fingers and down my cheeks. I felt Ed's arm round my shoulders and curled into him, sobbing my heart out. He squeezed my arm and I was reminded of those few weeks a while back when he and I had gone out. Not that it had amounted to much – just a few hugs and kisses, really. I cried harder. Ed hugged me properly. He was skinnier than Nico, but still broad and solid . . . comforting.

At last I pulled away, wiping under my eyes. Ed left the room, silently, and retrieved some toilet paper from the bathroom down the corridor. He handed me a length, then looked away as I blew my nose.

'It's bad, isn't it?' he said.

'What?' I sniffed. I looked up at him. He stared across the room.

'Whatever it is that you've seen in a vision that you

131

haven't told anyone.' He turned to me, almost looking me straight in the eye. 'I know what it's like to keep a secret, Ketty. I keep them all the time – whenever I mind-read someone and see their private thoughts and feelings.'

My chest tightened. 'I didn't see this in a vision . . .'

Ed nodded. He didn't speak. The atmosphere around us grew heavier. I stared at my lap.

'I can't tell you,' I whispered.

There was a long pause, then Ed cleared his throat. 'Well, if you can't tell me . . .' he said gently, 'maybe you could show me.'

I looked up, slowly, my heart beating fast, knowing what was coming.

Our eyes met.

Whoosh. It was like he was sucking my mind in on itself. And then his own consciousness was inside my head. I was trapped by it, held by it.

Don't worry. Ed's voice in my head was soft and soothing. *I'm only going to look at what you want me to see. Do you trust me?*

Yes. I thought the words. There was no way I could have spoken anyway, not unless Ed had let me.

Then show me what it is that's upsetting you so much.

I let the memory of my meeting with Foster and Lex at Highgate Cemetery and Foster's subsequent phone calls and demands flow through my thoughts.

And now Geri's sent the police to the wrong hospital and the bomb's going to go off at Gayton Hospital in South

London instead and I thought if I made an anonymous call and said I'd just seen Foster planting the Rainbow bomb, then . . .

Another whoosh and I felt Ed's consciousness withdraw from me. I blinked, finally able to speak. Ed was staring at me, his mouth open in horror.

'That hospital . . .' His voice was hoarse. 'All those people . . .'

'I know.' My eyes filled with tears again. 'That's why I want to call and say I'd seen Foster, but I don't even know what a Rainbow bomb looks like and if *you* don't know either, then—'

'I know enough.' Ed leaped to his feet. 'Come on.' He grabbed a school jumper that someone had left lying over a chair and shoved it into my arms. 'There's no signal down here. We'll have to go outside. Put this on. It's cold.'

I scurried after him, feeling bewildered. Ed was walking so quickly I almost had to run to keep up.

'I thought you said you didn't find out anything when you did your research?' I whispered as we made our way back through the main school building to the fire door closest to the front gates.

'Not when I looked on the internet. The 'Rainbow'-related stuff on there is all about these atomic weapons that were tested in space – when they exploded they created these coloured auras or something,' Ed whispered back. 'So I asked Geri. She explained that actual Rainbow bombs are small – no bigger than a pocket laptop – with coloured wires

133

hidden under a panel next to the timer. I don't have a picture but . . .'

'Coloured wires?' I said as we let ourselves quietly through the fire door. 'Is that where the nickname comes from, then? I mean "Rainbow"?'

'Yeah, you have to cut the wires in the order of the colours of the rainbow. Red first, then orange, and so on . . .'

I stopped in the cold night air as a thought struck me.

'Maybe *you* could make the call,' I said. 'You know more about the Rainbow bomb than me. And if Foster hears about a boy making an anonymous tip-off he'll know it wasn't me.'

'Er . . .' Ed rubbed his head. 'But I don't know what Foster looks like.'

'Yes you *do* – Geri showed us his picture last week. He's tall with dark, wavy hair and grey eyes. It doesn't matter anyway – you're not going to hang around to give a proper ID, are you?'

'I don't know . . .'

'*Please*, Ed.'

He looked at me, almost meeting my gaze, his own expression suddenly animated. 'How about if I say *I* planted the bomb,' he suggested. 'That way we don't need to worry about what Foster or the bomb look like. I'll just say it's there and ring off.'

My eyes widened. Why hadn't I thought of that?

'Brilliant idea,' I said.

Ed beamed. We crept round the corner to the back of the

134

kitchens. Ed took out his phone and dialled directory enquiries for Gayton Hospital's number.

I stood next to him as he phoned the hospital and, in the stillness of the night, could hear both sides of the conversation.

'Can I help you?' The receptionist sounded weary.

'Yes, er . . . I've just planted a bomb in your hospital,' Ed blurted out.

Silence. Then the receptionist spoke again, even more wearily. 'A bomb? Where?'

I frowned. That wasn't the reaction I'd been expecting. Why didn't the receptionist sound alarmed?

'I'm not going to tell you.' Ed said, a note of desperation creeping into his voice. 'But you have to evacuate the hospital, now.'

I held my breath.

'Your name, please.' The receptionist now sounded disdainful. And, still, completely unconcerned.

'I can't . . .' Ed frowned, glancing sideways at me.

'Hold the line.' Some ancient pop song replaced the receptionist's voice.

'I don't think she believes me,' Ed said, nervously.

I bit my lip. 'Wait and—'

'May I help?' A man's voice now. Stern and forbidding.

Ed gulped. He repeated what he'd told the receptionist.

'What's your name?' the man asked. 'How old are you?'

'I can't say . . .' Ed looked frantically round at me.

My heart thumped.

'Really.' The man sighed. 'Well, whoever you are, let me

135

tell you that yours is the fifth bomb scare call we've received tonight since that other hospital started evacuating. Do you have any idea how much these hoax calls cost us – and I don't just mean the money?'

'No,' Ed insisted, his voice rising. '*This* is the real bomb. Not the one at Linhurst.'

'OK then, give me your name and age and explain exactly where you are now and what you've done with this bomb of yours.'

'Well – it was someone else who planted the bomb,' Ed went on.

Shit.

'A friend of yours, is it?'

'No . . . yes . . . no . . .' Ed switched off his phone. Even in the gloom of the night I could see his face was bright red. He turned to me. 'I'm sorry, Ketty.'

I shook my head, my heart sinking. 'Don't . . .' I paused, as the only possible remaining course of action occurred to me. I checked the time. 'You know what we've got to do now?' I said.

'Yes, we have to call Geri. *You* have to. You have to tell her everything that's happened with Foster . . . how he's blackmailing you over Lex . . . how the real bomb is going to go off at Gayton Hospital in . . .' Ed checked his watch, '. . . in a couple of hours. And—'

'No.' I looked at him, my heart pounding. 'If I tell Geri everything then Foster will know I've grassed him up and Lex will die.'

'But all those people in the hospital . . .' Ed rubbed at his forehead. 'We can't just stand by and do nothing . . .'

'That's what I'm saying,' I went on, the words tumbling out of me. 'We have to go there . . . to Gayton Hospital. In person.'

Ed stared at me as if I were mad. 'But then *we'll* get blown up by the bomb. How does—?'

'I reckon if we hurry we should get there at least half an hour before the bomb's due to go off. You never know, we might see Foster and find a way to stop him. We don't know *when* he's planting the bomb, do we? And if everything else fails, we can still tell someone at the hospital face to face we've planted a bomb. Or *you* can. You can *mind-read* them into believing you.'

'You mean, like, *hypnotise* them? That's not how it works. I don't know if—'

'*Please*, Ed.'

'But what if they ask difficult questions again?'

'You can describe the bomb. You just told *me* all about it.'

'Okay.' Ed frowned. 'But if we go in person they'll know for sure how old we are and Foster is more likely to realise you've gone behind his back.'

'I *know* . . . it's a risk. But at least this way we stand a chance. Please, Ed. I can't do all this alone.'

For a second Ed hesitated. Then he set his mouth in a grim line.

'Okay,' he said. 'Let's go.'

We got a night bus from outside school into town. It took

ages. By the time we got to central London, it was almost light and the first underground trains were running. We sat, lost in our own thoughts, as the train headed south. Then we were off the tube and Ed had to consult his laptop again to find out where the hospital was exactly. So it was almost 5.40 a.m. by the time we turned the corner and saw it – a concrete jumble of assorted buildings – at the end of the road.

Flashing lights and a strong scent.

Dark corridors. Running. Foster's voice is in my head. 'Rick. It's all about Rick.'

The vision vanished. I swallowed. Maybe the corridors I kept seeing belonged to this hospital. And there were only fifteen minutes left until the bomb went off.

'Come on!' I grabbed Ed's arm, urging him on.

We broke into a run, and raced into the hospital car park. My heart was pounding. 'Let's go inside,' I panted. 'Just grab the first person we see.'

Ed nodded. The car park was virtually empty. We raced past a shed overflowing with bins to the main entrance. The hospital stretched out on either side, a mass of buildings.

We reached the wide, glass front door. I lifted my hand to push it open.

WHAM! The blast rocked the ground under our feet.

'Aaagh!' I grabbed Ed's arm, stumbling.

My whole being filled with horror. We were too late.

16: Silence

I spun round. Smoke was pouring out of the bin shed we'd just passed. Cars nearby screeched their alarms – the piercing noise filling the chilly dawn air. Shouts and screams echoed from the hospital – but the blast was definitely confined to the bin shed.

I stared wildly at Ed. Hadn't Geri said a Rainbow bomb was extremely powerful? He was gazing at the smoke, his mouth open.

'What happened?' I said. 'Was that the Rainbow bomb?'

A couple of paramedics rushed past us. People were appearing at windows along the side of the building. All eyes were on the smoke and the bin shed.

'I don't understand.' Ed shook his head, his mouth still gaping. 'A Rainbow bomb should have taken out the whole hospital.'

More people streaming into the car park now. The dawn hush completely blasted away. Ed grabbed my arm. 'Let's get out of here,' he said.

'But what about my warning . . .' As I said the words I realised they were pointless. I was too late. A bomb had already gone off here – how could it *not* be the Rainbow bomb?

'There's something wrong,' Ed said. 'But I don't understand what.'

'I know,' I said. 'Come on, before someone stops us.'

We raced out of the hospital car park. As we reached the nearby underground station my phone rang. *Nico calling.*

'I'm so glad it's you,' I said, the words tumbling out of me.

'It's not,' said a gruff voice. 'It's er . . . it's Mr Fox.'

'Oh.' I could feel my face reddening. 'Mr Fox . . . hi . . .'

'I've borrowed Nico's phone. Where *are* you, Ketty? Is Ed with you?'

I glanced sideways at Ed. He was leaning against the station entrance wall, rubbing his forehead and staring anxiously at me.

Oh God. 'Er . . . yes he is,' I went on. 'He's fine. We both are.'

'So where—'

'I got the hospital wrong,' I blurted out. 'I had another vision and realised it was Gayton Hospital in South London not Linhurst in the East End. So we came over here and—'

'You're in *South London*?' Mr Fox sounded incredulous. 'Why didn't you just find me or call Geri and *tell* us what you'd seen when you had this second vision?'

There was no answer to that without explaining about

Foster holding Lex hostage so I fell silent. Mr Fox sucked in his breath.

'I don't understand, Ketty, and I have to tell you I'm very concerned about this. For a start you're out of school in the middle of the night—'

'I know, sir.' *Oh, shit.* 'I'm really sorry, sir.'

'Get back here *immediately*.' Mr Fox rang off, sounding deeply troubled.

I felt sick all the way back on the tube. I'd let down Mr Fox who I liked . . . and Geri would be furious. Worst of all, I had no idea if Lex was still safe – or what Foster was really planning to do with him.

Geri herself was waiting outside the station, a stony expression on her face. She tugged her long, camel overcoat round her and opened the back door of her car. 'Get in,' she snapped.

Ed and I shuffled across the back seat. Geri got in beside us and directed her driver to take us back to Fox Academy.

'This has to stop, Ketty.' Her lips set in a thin line. 'If you see something in a vision the whole point is to *tell* me – not to act on your own.' She glanced across me at Ed. 'Or drag other people into your own reckless activities.'

'It wasn't Ed's fault,' I said. 'I made him come.'

Geri rolled her eyes. 'So what happened?'

I explained in more depth the version of events I'd already given Mr Fox.

'But I don't understand why the bomb at Gayton Hospital wasn't a Rainbow bomb,' I said.

'I'm afraid I do.' Geri turned to Ed. 'Do you have your laptop with you, Ed?'

'Yes.' He pulled it out of his backpack.

Geri took it and tapped at the keyboard for a few seconds. 'Our monitoring software picked this up about fifteen minutes ago.' She handed me the laptop and pointed to the screen. 'It explains everything.'

I gazed at the screen. A head shot of Foster. He was sitting in a chair – a relaxed pose with his legs loosely crossed and his head slightly tilted to one side.

'Hello.' As usual Foster's voice was smooth and menacing. 'By now you'll have realised that despite all your *special resources* I have had no trouble planting and detonating a bomb in a hospital.'

I glanced at Ed. He was staring at the screen, transfixed. What did Foster mean by *special resources*? Was that a coded reference to us . . . to the Medusa Project?

'However,' Foster went on, 'as you will also have realised, this was *not* the Rainbow bomb. That still remains in my possession. Whether or not it is used is up to the British government who have a choice to make.' He paused. 'My brother Rick is in prison for life for a crime he didn't commit. I have worked, tirelessly, for his release for the past two years. But all I encounter is bureaucracy and stonewalling. Nobody, it seems, is interested in miscarriages of justice any more. But maybe they'll be interested in a bomb which is capable of killing hundreds of people in one blast.'

My mind went back to the reply Foster had given me when I'd asked him why he was planning to bomb a hospital – *it's all about Rick* . . . Now it made sense.

I went back to the screen and Foster's broadcast. He was leaning forward in his chair, his face intent. 'These are my terms. You have forty-eight hours to release Rick to my care or innocent citizens will die. I've proved I can outwit you. Don't test my patience.' He leaned further forward, so his face filled the screen. His cold, grey eyes bored into me. 'A brother is a precious commodity. A brother's safety can be bought in many ways.' He smiled. 'The rest is silence.'

The screen fizzled black and grey.

I gasped. That last part of the message – about brothers – that was for *me*, I was sure. Specifically for me. Foster was telling me to keep quiet. Which meant . . . my heart leaped . . . that in spite of everything, there was still a chance for Lex.

'What does that mean?' Ed wrinkled his nose. '*The rest is silence*?'

'It's a line from a Shakespeare play . . . *Hamlet*,' Geri said briskly. 'No doubt Foster thought he'd round off with something suitably portentous to make sure we took him seriously.'

'So are you?' I said. 'Taking him seriously, I mean? Will the government let his brother go?'

'No.' Geri snapped the laptop shut and handed it back to Ed. 'The policy of this country is not to negotiate with terrorists. We're going to have to rely on all our intelligence sources to flush out Foster and his Rainbow bomb.' She looked at me quizzically. 'I don't understand how you got the hospital wrong – did you just mishear the name in your first vision?'

'I guess,' I muttered.

'And how on earth did you misunderstand about the bomb?' Geri went on. 'Why would you see Foster talking about setting off a Rainbow bomb when he was actually planning on using something much smaller?'

My face burned. 'Maybe he changed his mind,' I stammered.

'Or maybe Ketty sees different versions of the future. You know, alternate realities,' Ed added.

'Mmm.' Geri pursed her lips. 'It's certainly very disappointing.'

She turned and stared out of the window.

I glanced at Ed. I was grateful that he'd tried to cover for me, but privately I agreed with Geri. I mean, okay so I'd lied to her about both the hospital visions, but my ability *was* disappointing. It was ludicrously limited. Flaky, even. I should have been able to see what Foster was planning right from the start – but all my predictions came in fits and starts, making little sense out of context.

I didn't want to think about that. My mind wandered back to Lex. I hadn't stopped Foster from exploding his hospital bomb. Surely he'd release my brother now? I felt for the little troll doll in my pocket and rubbed it between my fingers like a worry bead. Staring out of the window at the dawn sky I tried again to have a vision, but I was too tired. My eyes ached from blinking, filling with tears that seemed to well up from the deepest loneliness I'd ever known.

The car drew up at Fox Academy's main entrance. It was still early. Most people at school would be getting up, maybe wandering down to breakfast in the canteen. In spite of everything, I was suddenly ravenously hungry.

Mr Fox, Nico and Dylan were standing by the front door. My heart thumped as I saw Nico. He looked gorgeous – his sleek hair slightly tousled, his school sweatshirt a little crumpled. I walked towards him, filling with relief. So long as Nico was with me, I could stand everything.

I smiled at him, soaking up his face – the olive skin, the way all the features sat in perfect symmetry. There were dark shadows under his eyes. I felt a stab of guilt that he must have been worrying about me.

'Hey.' I stood in front of him. The others were there too but I barely saw them. All I could see was Nico's dark eyes. They were boring into me, hard and questioning. Why wasn't he smiling back at me? The hunger that had been gnawing at my stomach just seconds before, vanished.

'Hey,' Nico said coldly. He glared from me to Ed, then back to me again. 'We need to talk.'

17: The truth

Nico glowered at me all through the debrief. Geri made me go through the whole sequence of events again – then asked Ed for his version.

Ed backed me up. He sounded guilty as hell while he was doing it but then that just looked like normal Ed – all shy and blushing and not looking anyone in the eye.

I soon realised what Nico was so upset about. Without being able to explain why I needed Ed's laptop it was impossible to make Nico understand why I'd asked Ed to go with me to the hospital instead of him.

Mr Fox told Ed and I that we were going to have to do our lessons as normal today, in spite of the fact that we must be tired after being up so much of the night. As soon as Geri dismissed us, with a severe warning for me and Ed about going off on our own again, Nico was by my side.

'Outside,' he hissed.

Oh, crap.

I followed him out into the Top Field. It was empty, as it

usually was at this time of the morning. Almost everyone in school was in the canteen, having breakfast. My heart pounded as Nico led me down to the tree where we used to meet up. We reached the tree and he turned to face me, his eyes cold.

'What's going on?' he said. 'You came to my dorm in the middle of the night and woke up Ed instead of *me*?'

'Yes, that's true,' I stammered, 'but I had a good reason and . . . and technically Ed was already awake when I got there.'

'Why did you want him with you instead of me?' Nico went on, his voice rising. 'Did you think his stupid mind-reading would be more useful than what I can do? Is it because you know sometimes my telekinesis goes out of control when you're around?'

'No.' I frowned. How could Nico even think that? 'No . . . I needed to borrow his laptop. There was something I wanted to look up on the internet.'

'In the middle of the night?' Nico's voice got even louder. 'Something that you couldn't find on one of the school's computers?'

I stared at him. *Oh, God . . . oh, God . . .*

'Well, say something, Ketty!' Nico was shouting now. He swore. 'Tell me, why you'd go off with Ed when you're supposed to be going out with me?'

'I'm sorry.' I stood, shivering, in the chilly morning air, uncertain how to explain. 'I was worried about my brother.'

'What's that got to do with it?' Nico snapped. 'You told me he was in France.'

I took a deep breath. I was going to have to tell him everything. It was the only way to make him understand – plus I was way too exhausted to come up with any more lies. I shivered, tugging my jumper closer round me. It was the one Ed had shoved at me in the basement music room – a pale blue school sweatshirt several sizes too big for me.

Nico mistook my hesitation for reluctance. His eyes flashed – dark and furious. 'Okay, if that's how you feel, then—'

'No, I'll explain.' I grabbed his arm. 'I'll explain everything.'

'Yeah?' he hissed. 'Then why don't you start with why you're wearing Ed's jumper?'

'It's not *his*—'

'Forget it, Ketty,' he snapped. 'I'm hungry. I'm going to get some breakfast.'

'Wait,' I said. 'Please, Nico, listen.'

He hesitated, staring at me.

'If Nico won't listen, you can tell *me* something.' It was Dylan, striding towards us across the grass, her green eyes cold and curious. Nico and I had been so caught up in our own conversation we hadn't even seen her coming.

She stopped. 'What I'm particularly interested in is where you *really* went yesterday when the rest of us were in Foster's office car park looking for that flash drive – and why all the data on it mysteriously emptied just after you used Ed's laptop.'

My stomach twisted into knots.

148

The three of us stood in silence for a second.

'Go on, then, Ketty,' Nico said quietly. 'Explain to both of us.'

I bit my lip. I didn't want to have to talk in front of Dylan but Nico was giving me no choice. I glanced at him . . . at the hurt behind the anger in his dark brown eyes.

'Foster is holding my brother hostage,' I said. The words sounded strange being said out loud. Flat, somehow, and unreal. 'He told me to delete the contents of that flash drive. He said if I didn't, he'd kill Lex.'

Nico and Dylan stared at me. The wind whistled around us. In the distance, in some other, ordinary universe, Tom was shouting at Curtis to hurry up or he'd eat all the sausages at breakfast.

Dylan gasped. 'No *way*.'

Nico looked at the grass.

'Foster also made me pretend to have a vision of him saying he was planting a Rainbow bomb at Linhurst Hospital at 6 a.m. this morning. I knew he was really planning on attacking Gayton Hospital, but I lied to everyone to save Lex.'

'Whoa,' Dylan said.

'And I couldn't stand it and . . . I ended up telling Ed because I was looking on his laptop for details of the Rainbow bomb. We went to Gayton Hospital to try and stop the bomb going off anonymously, but—'

'But you got there too late . . .' Dylan breathed.

'And the bomb at the hospital was only a bluff anyway,' I

149

added. 'Foster just wanted the government to see he meant business. He still has the Rainbow bomb and he still has Lex. He used me and now he wants me to keep quiet about it.'

'That is *sooo* heavy,' Dylan said.

I bit my lip. Nico looked at me with cold, hard eyes.

'I didn't have a choice,' I insisted. 'Do you understand?'

Nico shook his head. 'I understand that you lied to me about Lex being okay,' he said, coldly. 'And I understand that I was standing right next to you when you frigging faked that vision about a bomb being in a hospital.' He paused. 'Which means, I suppose, that what I understand most of all is that you don't trust me.'

Silence. I could feel Dylan beside us, watching, but I couldn't tear my eyes away from Nico. I'd never seen him look so angry. That icy look in his eyes terrified me far more than his earlier shouting.

'I *do* trust you,' I said, pleading with him now. 'I was just trying to protect you. I didn't want you to have to choose between me and all those people at the hospital being killed . . .'

'Yeah, right.' Nico strode off towards the school.

I darted after him, leaving Dylan behind. 'Nico, please . . . *please*.'

'Don't worry,' he said, marching on without looking at me. 'I'm not going to grass you up.'

I stared at him. How could he think that was what was on my mind right now?

'I'm so sorry I didn't tell you the truth,' I wept. 'I . . . I don't know what else to say.'

'Then try saying nothing. Make a nice change from your lies . . .'

'Nico—'

'Leave me alone.' Nico reached the school door and stormed through it.

I stood for a second, like I'd been punched in the guts. Then I took a step forward. I had to follow him. Try explaining again.

I felt a hand on my arm.

'I wouldn't.' It was Dylan. 'He's so mad right now that nothing you say will do any good.' She gazed at me, a disdainful look in her eyes.

'Guess you screwed things up big time,' she said.

For God's sake. 'Thanks for the newsflash.'

To my surprise, Dylan grinned. 'I kinda admire your guts, though.'

I stared at her. Was Dylan actually saying something that wasn't a sneer or an insult?

'I mean, I've never met anyone as determined as you . . . it's cool.'

I must have looked as astonished as I felt, because Dylan made a face.

'Don't look like that. I'm just saying "I get it". You're loyal to your brother. That's cool. You're prepared to do what it takes to make sure he's safe. That's about as cool as it gets.'

151

'Er . . . does that mean you won't tell Geri about me making stuff up?' I said.

'More than that,' Dylan said. 'It means I'll help you find Lex, if you want.'

'Really?' I stared at her. 'You'd do that?'

'Provided we also try and find out where Foster is *actually* going to detonate the Rainbow bomb.' Dylan twisted her hair round her hand. 'Look, I thought Geri was *all that* when I met her, but she's using us the same as everyone else. She's got a whole bunch of ambitions and we're just a way for her to make them happen. Now, personally, I love having the Medusa gene and being able to protect myself with my Gift. And I used to think going on missions would be cool. But Geri's just using us. And as for Uncle Fergus and his trust games . . .' She shook her head.

I stared at her. It was funny hearing Dylan refer to Mr Fox as her uncle. I'd completely forgotten his brother, William Fox, the creator of the Medusa Gene, was her dad.

'Thanks,' I said.

'No sweat.' Dylan smiled, revealing her perfectly even, white teeth. 'So I guess that predicting the future thing you do is the key, isn't it? Tell me how it works.'

'I don't really know,' I admitted, shoving my hands in my pockets. 'I mean my visions can happen anywhere, at any time . . . I don't know what brings them on, though I can *make* them happen now. Hey . . .' I felt the troll doll in my pocket. 'Maybe I could specifically try to focus on something of Lex's *before* I go into the vision. That might help me see where he is.'

'Sure.' Dylan's eyes widened. 'Let's go somewhere and try it.'

But just then the bell rang for first period and other students swarmed into the corridor. Tom, Lola and Curtis were among the crowds heading towards us. Tom and Curtis's eyes latched onto Dylan as they approached. Like all the other boys in our year they appeared to have a major crush on her – not that she'd shown the slightest interest in any of them.

'Damn,' I said. 'We'll have to meet later.'

Dylan made a face. 'Okay.' She paused. 'Recess. The art department. See ya.'

And she was gone. I hurried to my own class, my head spinning with what had just happened. Dylan was actually being friendly for once!

I forgot about her in maths. Nico was there, completely ignoring me, which made me miserable again. I couldn't concentrate on anything Mr Rogerson said. Luckily, he didn't notice. He had his hands full controlling his hair – he wore a hairpiece on top and every now and then Nico moved it a fraction by telekinesis so it looked as if it had slipped slightly. Another time I would have laughed. Right now, it was all I could do not to cry.

Then it was English, with Ed, where I actually fell asleep on my desk while we were supposed to be doing a test. After that, break.

Ed and I had just left our classroom when Dylan materialised in front of us.

'Let's go. And Ed should come too,' she said imperiously. 'He's good at analysing stuff. See you in five.' She swept off.

I glanced at Ed. 'You up for that?'

'Er . . . sure,' he nodded, blinking nervously. 'Where are we going?'

'Art department,' I said, walking off.

The room was empty when we got there. Ed and I made our way through to the techy bit – full of work tables with blowtorches and bits of engineering equipment. Dylan was waiting by the sink. I shut the door through to the main art room. The distant sounds of voices and footsteps faded away.

'Okay then, Little Miss Grungy Sweats . . .' Dylan grinned. 'Let's go.'

I stared at her.

'Bring it on,' she urged. 'Have a vision.'

I took a deep breath and took the blond troll doll out of my pocket. I clutched it in my hand and tried to picture my brother. The lanky blond hair framing that crooked, gap-toothed smile.

I turned my face towards the strip light in the ceiling and focused on imagining the sweet, heavy smell that always accompanied my visions. Trying to forget that Ed and Dylan were watching, I started blinking.

Dark corridors. Running. On and on. I glance beside me. Dylan is there. Running too. I'm scared . . . I'm looking for something . . .

154

I snapped out of it. Dylan was peering at me, her eyes sparkling.

'Wow, that is *neat*,' she said. 'Your eyes go all glassy, it's real freaky. What did you see?'

'Nothing . . . some corridors. You were there.' *God*, Nico had seen me like this, several times. Did I really look like a freak?

Dylan nodded. 'Okay, so you can bring on the visions. But you need to be able to see more . . . to control what and when you see stuff. Why don't you try telling yourself to see into a particular place – or a time, like . . . like this afternoon maybe . . .'

'Er . . . it doesn't work like that. I mean, I don't have any control over what comes up. It's like I'm just watching it – like a film playing in my head.'

I glanced at Ed, blushing, hoping he would understand.

He looked at me, avoiding meeting my eyes as usual. 'Do you really want to control your visions more?' he said. 'Wouldn't you rather just not have them at all?'

I stared back at him. 'Of course. But as I *do* have them, I have to use them if . . . when . . . it can help people.'

Ed fell silent. Dylan prodded him. 'Freakin' hell, Chino Boy, ask her some *helpful* questions, will you?'

'Okay.' Ed frowned. 'I was . . . er . . . I was wondering . . .'

Dylan rolled her eyes impatiently. 'Go on.'

'Are you always *in* the visions?' Ed asked. 'I mean, can you see stuff that happens when you're *not* around, or are you always there when it's happening?'

'I've never really thought about it,' I said, 'but I guess I *am* always there. I mean all the visions I've had – from the little flashes to the big sequences – they've been of people and places and events that I went on to see in real life within a few days.'

Ed nodded. Dylan's eyes glittered.

'That's *sooo* amazing,' she said.

'What I really want a chance to find out,' I said, 'is whether I can *change* the future once I've seen it.'

'Of course you can't,' Ed said.

We both stared at him. His face reddened. 'I just don't see how that could be possible. I know I said all that stuff about alternate realities to Geri, but it's not actually logical. If you've seen something is going to happen, how can it *not* happen?'

'Because it's just one version of the future – one possibility . . .' I said.

'Do you really think that?' Ed asked.

I looked at the glass-fronted cupboards of the design and technology room. They were full of implements – saws, welding irons, pliers. Everything you needed to make real, tangible stuff. Nothing that helped with what went on inside people's heads.

Especially mine.

'I don't know.' I looked at them and, suddenly, tears filled my eyes. 'I just don't know.'

Ed made a sympathetic face.

Dylan clapped her hands. 'Never mind that, do another

vision. See what happens. This time tell yourself you're going to see what happens when we walk out of this room. Like . . . like who we're going to see first . . .'

Oh God. It was hard enough just bringing on another vision. There was certainly no way I could control what I saw. As soon as the flashing lights started for real, I was there, in those same corridors again. I tried to detach, to tell myself I didn't want these pictures.

But my brain obviously wasn't listening.

'It's no good,' I complained as the vision ended. 'Just more corridors. I don't even know where they are – it's all too dark and hazy.'

The bell went for the end of break. My eyes filled with tears again. I was tired. I couldn't control my visions. And my next lesson was history – where I would definitely see Nico again and have to deal with him looking at me like I was a piece of slime.

'Okay, so the visions aren't getting us anywhere, but we're still going to find your brother and stop the Rainbow bomb,' Dylan insisted. 'We just have to work out another way of doing it. Let's meet next recess.' She picked up her bag and swung it over her shoulder. As she made for the door, Ed touched my hand. To my surprise he was looking right at me. Right into my eyes.

With a whoosh, he was inside my head. *You know what you said about having to use your abilities if or when it could help people?*

I thought my answer – *yes.*

Well, I've got an idea . . . how about I mind-read Foster and find out where he's both keeping Lex and planning to set off the Rainbow bomb?

Ed broke the link between us, looking away towards the door where Dylan was standing, glancing over her shoulder at us.

'What are you doing?' she said. 'What's going on?'

I stared at Ed's red face. Was he really prepared to do that?

'But that means using your powers,' I stammered. 'Which Foster knows about . . . it would be dangerous just getting close to him . . .'

'What would?' Dylan demanded from the door.

Then Ed met my eyes again.

If I could do it, it would save everyone that the Rainbow bomb would kill.

But you could be hurt . . . The thought forced its way to the front of my mind.

And you'd care?

Of course I would, Ed – I love you . . . like a brother.

There was a long pause while Ed gazed into my eyes. He was still inside my head, but I could sense his mind resting, not probing mine.

Waiting. Until . . . *Then it would all be worth it, whatever happens.* He tore his gaze away.

I sat down on the edge of the tech table, my heart pounding.

'What was *that* about?' Dylan was walking towards us, her hands on her hips.

158

'Ed had an idea . . .' I mumbled.

'It's more than an idea,' Ed said, his face breaking into a grim smile. 'It's a plan, but it'll need all three of us for it to work.'

18: Finding Foster

I took a deep breath and dialled the number for Foster's company. It was lunch break now – a brilliantly sunny afternoon. Ed, Dylan and I were sitting outside by the trees where I'd called Lex after that first vision on Monday. I felt like I'd lived a million lifetimes since then.

I lifted my hand to shield my face from the glare as I waited for the receptionist at Fostergames to answer. Dylan was leaning against a tree next to me, her long hair hidden under a blue cap. Ed tapped his fingers nervously on the grass beside him.

I hadn't seen Nico since the maths lesson where he'd completely ignored me.

A woman answered. 'Fostergames Limited. How may I help you?'

'I'd like to speak to Damian Foster' PA, please,' I said, as firmly as I could.

Dylan had coached me beforehand on the importance of sounding confident. I didn't really like her bossing me around on that any more than I had over my visions, but I knew she was right.

'Hold the line.'

The phone rang again.

'Fostergames Limited. Anita speaking.' The speaker sounded fraught.

'Hi.'

I glanced at Dylan. She was staring at me, her green eyes glittering. Ed was still tapping his fingers on the grass beside him.

'Could I speak to Damian Foster, please,' I said, trying to keep my voice steady.

'He's not in the office. I'm his PA.' She hesitated. 'Actually it's all a bit chaotic here . . .'

I nodded. Geri had told us that the police had gone back to Foster's offices as soon as his broadcast was streamed on the internet. This time they were openly requisitioning computers *and* interrogating the workforce for clues. There was a warrant out for Foster's arrest too.

I blew out my breath. 'Okay,' I said. 'Well, if you speak to him, please tell him I called.'

'Er . . . what's your name? What's it about?' I could hear the frown in the PA's voice.

'Tell him it's Ketty from Medusa.'

A pause, then the line went dead.

I put my phone down.

'What happened?' Dylan sat forward. 'Is he calling back?'

'I don't—' My phone rang. I stared at it. *Number withheld*.
'Hello?'

'What the hell are you doing calling my office number?'
Foster sounded irate. 'The police are monitoring all calls in,
trying to work out where I am. May I remind you that it's
not in your best interests to help them find me, Ketty. Any
moves on me, and your brother's dead.'

My heart raced. 'Is Lex okay?'

'Yes. What do you want?'

'You said you'd let Lex go once I told the lie about where
the Rainbow bomb was.'

'No. I said I'd let him go once I'd got what I want. I'll
release him as soon as *my* brother's released. Until then, all
you have to do is keep quiet.'

I hesitated. Now I was actually talking to Foster our
whole plan seemed ultra complicated. Maybe I *should* do
what Foster said. At least it was clear-cut. Except . . . Foster
had changed the deal before. He could change it again. I
had absolutely no guarantee he was *ever* going to let Lex
go. And he'd made it quite clear I couldn't trust him an
inch.

I took a deep breath.

'What if I tell you all about Medusa? What if I tell you
everything Geri Paterson, the head of the Medusa Project, is
planning? She's the one who first worked out you were
hacking into the MoD database . . . who sent us to the car
park where the others found the flash drive with the Gayton
Hospital schematic.'

'And why would that interest me?'

'Because Geri Paterson is the link between us and the government,' I said, trying to keep my voice even. 'She knows everything the government security agents are planning – how they're hoping to trap you and find the Rainbow bomb . . .'

'How do you know so much about what's going on inside Ms Paterson's head?' Foster's voice was suddenly calm and cold.

I glanced at Ed. He had stopped tapping his fingers on the grass and was staring, intently, at the ground. He felt my gaze and looked up, not quite meeting my eyes.

'My . . . er . . . it's my friend. In Medusa. He can read people's minds,' I explained. 'He's seen everything that Geri Paterson knows – and more.'

A pause. 'Is this the same boy you were with at the Rufus Stone?'

'No, that's Nico. His ability is telekinesis. We all have the same gene but it turned out differently in each of us,' I went on. 'Ed's prepared to tell you what he's seen – Geri Paterson's thoughts – in order to help me . . . in order to get Lex back.' I hesitated, my heart now pounding. 'Will you . . . do we have a deal?'

A few long seconds ticked by. The sun blazed down. Dylan and Ed sat, intent, beside me. A fly buzzed past.

And then Foster spoke. 'Yes, we have a deal. We'll meet this evening. There's a funfair at Hampstead Heath tonight. That should provide enough cover. Bring your friend . . . Ed.

Only Ed. Seven p.m. Dodgems. And don't even *think* about double-crossing me. I won't be bringing Lex – but if you give me the information you're promising, I'll take you to him.'

He rang off. I turned to the others.

'It's done.'

Ed nodded, his forehead creased with worry lines.

I felt a stab of guilt at what he was offering to do. 'Are you sure about this, Ed?'

'Course he is.' Dylan jumped to her feet. 'Come on. We've got to work out how we're going to get away once Ed breaks the link with Foster.'

Ed nodded. 'We'll have to move fast. Once I let go of the connection he'll be able to move and speak and—'

'It'll be fine,' Dylan insisted. 'Won't it, Ketty?'

I nodded, but inside my guts were tied up in knots. All this would be so much easier if Nico was with us. He could make sure we got away okay. Ed stood up and held out his hand to help me up.

'Don't worry, Ketty,' he said as we followed Dylan back to the school building. 'I'll find out where Lex *and* the bomb are. Then all we'll have to do is phone Geri and tell her you've seen both things in another vision.'

I nodded. It sounded simple. But my guts were still knotted and my throat felt tight. I knew just how dangerous Foster was. If anything went wrong, all three of us could easily end up dead.

I spent the rest of the day feeling just as bad. I could

164

barely follow what the teachers were saying in any of my lessons, on top of which Nico was acting like I didn't exist, picking seats as far away from me as possible in every class we had together that afternoon.

By 4 p.m. I was completely exhausted. Ed made me go upstairs and lie down in my dorm. I didn't think I'd sleep but I did. Dylan had to wake me up in the end.

'Uncle Fergus has called us for another of those real ridiculous "trust" training sessions at seven tomorrow morning,' she said as I splashed some water on my face. 'Apparently this time we're going to stand in a circle with our eyes closed and catch each person in turn as they fall backwards.' She made a face. 'You know, I don't have much time for Geri, but at least she's got a grip on the real world!'

I didn't say anything. I didn't like to diss Mr Fox but I had to admit Dylan had a point when it came to the training we were being given. It was all very well for Nico – his telekinesis gave him a ready-made weapon. But Dylan could only protect herself if she saw a physical threat coming – while Ed and I needed all the help we could get, both in attack and defence skills.

'I wish we'd had more training too,' I said, pulling on my trainers. I still felt tired, but my body felt weirdly strung out too – tense and tight. What I really needed was a run to wind down. Not that there was any chance of that right now.

'You and Ed'll be awesome,' Dylan said, wandering over to her own bed. The area around it was the messiest in the dorm, if not the whole school. Dylan was constantly getting detention for not tidying up. Not that she seemed to care. 'I'm going to stand real close. Foster doesn't know what I look like. If he tries anything I'll be able to get there fast and . . . Hey, Ketty . . .' She pulled a pale blue jacket from the cupboard by her bed. 'Why don't you try this on?'

'*Me?*' I stared at the jacket. It was smart, fitted into the waist and slightly cropped, like most of Dylan's tops. 'Wear *that*?'

'Sure.' Dylan flicked her hair over her shoulder and held the jacket out towards me. 'You'd look real good in more tailored clothes . . . better than you do in those old sweats anyway.'

I frowned. 'I *like* comfortable clothes,' I said, feeling indignant. What was Dylan *doing*? We were on the verge of a major and secret mission, risking our own lives to save my brother's – and she was offering me fashion advice.

'Yeah, I kinda got that you like dressing like a bum.' Dylan laughed. 'But you'd look awesome in something like this.'

'Don't you think the whole point of this evening is that we *don't* stand out too much?' I said, trying to get as much ice in my voice as possible. *Jesus*, I got enough of that kind of interfering crap from my mum whenever she saw me.

'Whatever.' Unperturbed, Dylan dropped the jacket on her bed. 'Come on. Ed's waiting downstairs.'

It took us nearly an hour to get to Hampstead Heath. On the way, I tried to summon a vision of the next couple of hours, but all I kept seeing were those same, dark corridors from before. In the end I gave up and focused on what I was going to have to do once we met Foster at the dodgems – introduce Ed and let him hook into Foster's mind.

The rest of the plan was simple. Once Ed had the information on Lex and the bomb he would break the connection. My job was to get him and myself away, fast. Dylan would do the rest – drawing Foster's fire while we got to safety and called Geri. I was sure that, whatever else Geri did, she would at least make sure Lex was rescued.

The streets around Hampstead Heath were busy with people heading for the funfair. Dylan strode ahead, turning every head as she passed in her jeans and cropped green jumper.

Ed shuffled along beside me. He wasn't saying much but I could tell from the way his shoulders were hunched and his hands shoved deep inside his trouser pockets that he was extremely nervous. I glanced round as we walked down a dirt track. No sign of Foster – just hordes of people: families, groups of teenagers, couples, all laughing and smiling at the funfair rides.

Suddenly I had the sense we were being watched. I'd had it before, both when we got on and off the underground. I shook myself. I was just being paranoid. Foster probably wasn't even here yet.

We passed a carousel, some smaller kids' rides, then a couple of bigger, faster ones. Amusement stands were everywhere, selling candyfloss and those giant teddy bears you get if you hook the right-numbered duck with a pole. Fairy lights sparkled along the sides of the stands and the air was filled with the smell of generators and hot dogs and the sound of ancient rock tracks, half muffled by the wind.

I had a sudden memory of a very different funfair – the one where I'd won the troll doll for Lex. It was almost a year ago, before I'd started at Fox Academy. Mum and Dad were over on a visit and Lex and I had walked through the funfair to meet them for lunch.

Mum and Dad had been in a good mood. Normally when we saw them everything was fine for about thirty minutes and then the old tensions would start up again. But for once that didn't happen . . . Dad *didn't* lecture Lex about going to uni and Mum *didn't* nag me about my clothes being scruffy or try to persuade me I should stop spending so much of my time running and 'take that string out of your hair and do something fun, darling, like ballroom dancing'.

Back then, the sun had shone and I hadn't even heard of the Medusa gene. I sighed, turning my attention back to today where the light was just fading and a cool evening breeze rippled across the Heath.

As we reached the waltzer, Dylan stopped. 'I can see the dodgems a couple of rides down,' she said. 'We might as well wait here a minute, once we go closer I won't be able to talk to you.' Something behind me caught her eye and she looked up.

I checked the time. Ten minutes to go until the meeting with Foster.

And then a hand grabbed my arm.

19: A revelation

'What the hell kind of plan is this?' Nico's voice hissed in my ear.

I spun round. It was him. Really him. My mouth fell open.

Nico drew me aside and lowered his voice. 'Were you leaving me out *again*, Ketty?'

I stared at him. All the sights and sounds of the funfair disappeared. I completely forgot Dylan and Ed, standing nearby, and the meeting with Foster in just a few minutes' time.

All I could see were Nico's deep, dark eyes and his smooth, olive-skinned face. A strand of hair fell over his cheek. He brushed it away.

'Well?' he said.

Was he still angry? Why would he be here if he was still angry?

'You . . . you wouldn't talk to me . . .' I stammered. 'I *couldn't* ask you to be part of this, you wouldn't speak to—'

'Only because you didn't trust me.'

'I told you, I was trying to protect you.'

We stood silently for a second. A couple of kids shrieked past us, fighting over a candyfloss stick. And then Nico's eyes softened.

'I know.' His voice was heavy. 'Ed told me that too . . . at the end of our French class. Then Dylan found me between lessons and said I was a jerk for not listening to you. They both seemed to think I should be here to help.'

I followed Nico's gaze to where the others were standing. Ed was half turned away, looking embarrassed. Dylan was staring straight at us, an ironic glint in her eye.

I stood, letting what Nico had said sink in. The others had spoken to him . . . asked him to come with us . . .

'So Ed and Dylan *knew* you were following us?' As I said the words, I remembered the sense I'd had earlier that we were being watched.

'No,' Nico said. 'I mean, I said I'd think about it but they didn't know. I guess they didn't want to say anything to you in case I didn't show up.'

'So . . . so you're just here because of Ed and Dylan . . .' I said slowly, 'because they asked you to come?'

A heavy feeling settled in the pit of my stomach. It was good he was here, of course. Good for Dylan. Particularly good for Ed, who was going to be in the most vulnerable position. And yet, when I'd seen Nico I'd hoped that, just maybe, he'd come along because he'd forgiven me. Because he wanted us to be together again.

'That's not the whole reason.' A grin crept across Nico's face.

My heart jumped with hope. Did that mean it was partly for me? I moved closer, everything else forgotten, my eyes straining to read his expression.

'I'm still mad at you for not telling me, though . . .' Nico's grin widened. 'What were you thinking? You won't stand a chance on your own against Foster. You might as well be armed with flowers. I mean Dylan can help, but—'

'So you're saying I'm incompetent?' I beamed at him.

'No, I'm saying you're the most stubborn person I've ever met.' Nico laughed and my heart flipped over in my chest and suddenly I knew why I hadn't wanted Ed to know Nico and I were together. It *was* partly to spare Ed's feelings. But it was mostly because I was scared.

Scared of admitting to anyone how much I liked Nico.

Scared of admitting it to myself.

I glanced at the time again. Still six minutes until Ed and I were due to meet Foster.

Dylan came over, arms folded.

'Is it time?' Nico asked.

'Let's get in position,' she said.

'Right.' Ed looked nervous, though he was clearly relieved now Nico was here.

'Wait. There's something I want to tell you both.' I took a deep breath. 'Nico and I are going out together. At least we are if he still wants to.'

171

There. I'd said it.

I waited for their shocked reactions, my face burning.

But to my astonishment, Dylan just rolled her eyes. 'Like *that's* a surprise to anyone.'

I glanced at Ed.

'It *was* kind of obvious, Ketty . . .' He shrugged. His face was bright red. 'I mean everyone at school assumed you two were together at the beginning of term.'

What? I stared harder at him, willing him to look at me properly. He met my eyes and with that, now familiar, sucking feeling he was inside my head.

My thoughts reared up before I could stop them: *I thought you'd be cross or upset that I was going out with Nico so soon after breaking up with you.*

Not cross. And only upset for a bit, because you deserve the best. I never thought you'd go out with me for long, anyway. Ed's thought was measured and careful. I had the strong sense he was holding something back, but he broke the connection and turned, immediately, to Dylan, asking her some detail about how close to Foster she was planning to stand.

I looked up at Nico.

'What did Ed "say" just then?' he whispered. He sounded wary, but not jealous.

'He just said I deserved the best,' I whispered back.

'You do, babe.' Nico grinned. 'What d'you think *I* am?'

I couldn't help but grin back. And yet the whole thing still didn't quite make sense.

'So if everyone knew about us, why didn't anyone say anything?' I asked, quietly.

'Maybe because it's not really that big a deal to anyone else.'

I let this sink in.

'Come *on*, it'll be fine,' Dylan said to Ed. She turned to me and Nico and pointed towards the dodgems. 'We should go. Ed and Ketty need to be waiting for Foster by the cars. I'm going to hang by that cotton candy stall. Nico – you get behind a tree and get ready in case you have to do your thing.'

'Bossy as ever, I see,' Nico murmured as we followed her.

'Everyone already knows about us?' I whispered. '*Really*?'

Nico squeezed my hand. 'Like I said, it's not that much of a big deal to anyone else . . .' He paused. 'Just to me.'

I stopped, my heart beating fast. 'And me,' I said.

We looked at each other for a second. Then Nico shook himself.

'Go with Ed,' he ordered. 'And be careful. I'll be over there.' He pointed at a nearby tree, squeezed my hand again, then sped off.

I walked on to the dodgems. The cars were waiting to race, music blasting out over the PA. As I reached Ed, my phone rang.

It was Foster.

'Change of plan,' he said smoothly. 'I'm at the big wheel. Go there, now.'

20: Big wheel

Ed was shaking as we approached the big wheel. As the tallest ride at the funfair it was easy enough to spot at the end of a big row of amusement arcade style stands. The two-minute walk over here had strung out every nerve in my body. I hadn't dared look round to see if I could spot either Nico or Dylan. They must both have seen me take the phone call – and as they hadn't rushed over when Ed and I started walking away from the dodgems, I could only assume they were watching us still.

Foster was waiting beside the queue for the ride. There were at least ten sets of people waiting to get on as the big wheel slowly turned, offloading and reloading its passengers.

'Hello, Ketty.' Foster met my gaze, his expression calm and even. 'And this must be Ed.' He held out his hand.

Ed shook it, carefully keeping his eyes away from Foster's.

Foster looked round. 'I see no police . . .' He gave us a

thin-lipped smile. 'No adult agents . . . Well done. Now let's take a ride.'

'What?' Startled, I glanced at the big wheel behind us. 'On that?'

'No.' Ed's voice shook. He rubbed his forehead.

'Yes.' Foster gripped my wrist. 'We can't talk in front of all these people and you're a pair of idiots if you think I'm going anywhere more private with that other friend of yours roaming around – Nico. Yes, I'm sure he's here somewhere, so don't bother denying it.'

I glanced sideways at the queue. It was still long. At least that gave us a bit of time. Ed's face was white.

But Foster gave my wrist a tug. 'Come on.' He pushed me towards the head of the queue. 'We don't have to wait.'

I stumbled the few steps it took to reach the base of the wheel, Ed beside me. A greasy-haired girl was collecting tokens, then allowing passengers onto the wheel. As we reached her, Foster slipped a note into her palm. The girl pocketed the cash and shoved us forward, ahead of the people at the head of the queue, ignoring their protests.

Foster pushed me into the seat. It was low and free-swinging, with a bar that lowered in front. I sat down hard on the cold metal. Foster placed himself beside me, pulling Ed in after him.

The greasy-haired girl shoved the bar in front of us down. It clicked into place just over our legs. The seat lurched. Someone in the queue behind gave a low grumble but the girl muttered something and they shut up.

The seat swung upwards. The air was cooler now, away from everyone. I sat, stunned, for a second. How had everything happened so fast?

I looked past Foster and a terrified Ed, down to the ground. I spotted Dylan straight away, her red hair like a beacon in a sea of brown and black. The wheel stopped for a moment, letting on its last set of passengers, then began its slow rotation again.

Foster sat back. 'You have approximately two minutes, Ed. I suggest you tell me what you know.'

Ed's face was as white as his knuckles, clutching the bar in front. He didn't look capable of speech, let alone mind-reading. My heart pounded. I could almost feel the adrenalin surge as we reached the top of the wheel's range. North London was spread out around us. Tiny trees and roads and houses that looked like they belonged to dolls. Over to the north-east I could see what I guessed must be Alexandra Palace then, beyond that, a row of skyscrapers.

'Ed?'

He didn't reply. My heart was thumping against my chest now. Lights flashed in front of my eyes. A sweet heavy smell filled the air. A vision was coming. *No.* I fought it back, trying to calm my breathing. But the force of it was too huge. Too strong.

Corridors again. Can't see where. Running. Dylan beside me. It's dark. It's night time.

I snapped out of the vision. So *that* was why I hadn't been able to see those corridors properly. I was running through them at night, in the dark.

I glanced hurriedly over at Foster. He was still waiting for Ed to speak. He hadn't noticed my eyes glaze over.

'*Ed*,' I said again, more forcefully. 'Do it.'

Ed nodded. He wiped his sweaty hands on his chinos. Then he looked up, right into Foster's eyes.

Foster stiffened, his gaze losing its focus. Ed had him.

'You have to hold him like that until we get back down,' I said.

'I know.' Ed's voice wavered. 'Damn, this is hard.'

'What? Why?'

But Ed didn't reply. I turned my attention to the ground. I found Dylan again. A tiny dot, standing with her face upturned towards us. Nico was beside her, also looking up. The wheel began its descent.

Down, round, up and down again.

Ed was frowning, his forehead creased with lines.

I suddenly realised what a vulnerable position we were in. Once Ed broke the connection at the end of the ride, we were going to have to move fast to get away from Foster.

I chewed on my lip. Ed was very pale now – and still frowning. It looked like he was having some sort of problem reading Foster.

Oh, God, oh God.

The wheel reached the bottom of its axis and swung forward again. I caught sight of Dylan and Nico again, their faces anxious. Adrenalin surged through me again as the wheel got higher. Flashing lights sparkled in front of my eyes. *No.* I tried to stop the vision, but it was too strong.

177

Corridors. I'm running. I'm scared. Turning corners. Dylan beside me. I can hear her footsteps . . . her shallow breathing . . . Up ahead a room. I have to get in there. There's something inside I have to reach. Closer. I grab the door.

I snapped out of the vision, gasping for breath.

The wheel was at the very top of its climb. We swung for a second, then moved down again. We stopped with a jolt. My stomach lurched. The people in the seats in front were squealing with delight. Down below, one of the big wheel compartments was emptying and being refilled with new passengers. That meant the ride was over, didn't it . . . we'd be able to get off in a minute.

Ed was still frowning, his breath rapid and jerky. He didn't look good. His face was completely drained of colour, his eyes in agony. I suddenly realised he wouldn't last until we reached the bottom. That Foster was making something about the mind-reading too difficult for him.

The wheel swung down again, then stopped. More passengers below got out. Three more stops until it was our turn.

I *had* to find some way of restraining Foster so Ed could break free.

I looked round frantically. There was nothing in the seat area to help. I stared at the bar over our laps. Maybe if I could tie Foster to that, then Ed could break the connection. *Yes.* Foster would be held fast, Ed could get his breath back and we'd have a head start for getting away once we were back on the ground.

What could I use to tie Foster up with? I glanced at my own clothes. Nothing. I looked at Ed. His chinos were fastened with a slim brown leather belt. *There.* I reached past Foster and unbuckled the belt. The seat swung crazily as I tugged at the belt, yanking it through the loops in Ed's trouser waistband. I could feel his body tensing as I worked.

'I'm going to tie Foster up,' I explained. 'Then you can break free.'

The wheel lowered again. We swung to a standstill. Two more stops.

Ed groaned. What was Foster *doing* to him?

At last the belt came completely free. I looped it round the bar in front of us, then took Foster's hands and wound the belt tightly round his wrists. I tied it in three knots, tugging as hard as I could. Now Foster was tied to the bar. When the bar rose he would still be held there, while we got away. Of course Foster would be able to work the belt loose eventually, but it should give us a bit of time.

'It's okay, Ed, you can end the connection.'

Ed groaned again. His face was screwed up with concentration. 'I *can't*,' he gasped.

One more stop.

'You *have* to.' My voice rose in panic. 'We're going to have to get off in a second.'

With a roar, Ed tore his eyes away from Foster. And then everything happened at once.

Ed retched. He leaned forward, hanging over the bar and

heaving like he was going to vomit. Foster yelled. A huge, frustrated roar of pure rage. He tugged at the belt tying his wrists to the bar in front, then turned on me, shouting and swearing at me to undo it.

I shrank back in the corner as the wheel stopped again, then swung forward once more. The few seconds it took to reach the bottom seemed an eternity. As we stopped again, our feet finally on solid ground, Foster stopped yelling. His whole body pulsed with rage. I shrank further away, trembling.

Ed sat back, his face ashen.

The greasy-haired girl from before walked over. She stared at Ed, open-mouthed. 'You okay, love?' the girl asked.

Ed nodded.

Still looking at him, the girl grabbed the bar and lifted it off us. Foster hands, still tied to the bar, rose as she did so.

'Help me, please,' he said politely. 'My niece and nephew have played a prank.'

The girl stared, dully, at his tied wrists. 'What the—?'

I was already up and squeezing past Foster. I grabbed Ed's hand and hauled him off the big wheel. As I pushed past the girl, Nico appeared.

'Jesus Christ, Ketty—'

'Come *on*, let's get Ed out of here.'

Nico hooked one of Ed's arms around his shoulder and half carried, half dragged him away from the ride. Dylan was at the base of the big wheel steps, pushing people back to let us through.

I staggered down after Nico and Ed. The whole funfair seemed more crowded than before. I couldn't work out where I was or where we should go. Dylan was racing ahead. My legs shook as I tried to follow her. I'd had jelly legs before, but only after pushing myself really hard in a long run. This was different, this was from the shock, my whole body trembling.

Keeping Nico and Ed in my sights I stumbled on. The crowd was thinner now. My legs grew more used to carrying me. I ran faster. Past the boys. We emerged into a small field surrounded on three sides by trees.

A roar in my ear. Foster came from nowhere. He leaped in front of me, hand outstretched. He grabbed at my hair but in the split second it took him to lunge forward, Dylan was there, thrusting her own arm between me and Foster. His hand punched into hers but lost its force as it made contact. Just a gentle tap.

Dylan grinned. Foster stared at her, shocked.

Nico gave an angry yell. He focused for a second . . . lifted his hand . . . Foster went flying backward, landing on his side in the mud.

Nico stared at him, panting.

I looked round. No one else was here. No one was watching us.

Dylan hooked Ed's limp arm over her shoulder. 'I got you,' she said.

Foster struggled up.

Nico raised his hand again. 'You bastard,' he hissed.

Foster's head fell back into the mud.

'Come on.' I found my voice at last.

The others all looked at me. I pointed to the nearby line of trees.

'In there,' I said. 'Run.'

21: Mixed messages

Several long seconds later we reached the cover of the trees. I looked back. Foster was struggling to his feet, wiping mud from his face. A family wandered past, the mother pulling her children out of his way.

Foster looked round. But the light was almost gone now and we were well hidden by the trees.

'He hasn't seen us,' Dylan said.

'Ketty?' Nico's anxious voice made me turn.

He was standing over Ed who was kneeling amid twigs and grass and fallen leaves, rocking to and fro.

'What's the matter with him?' Nico asked.

I ran over and knelt beside Ed. He was moaning, white-faced and clutching his stomach. 'Ed?' I stroked his back. 'Ed, what is it?'

For answer, Ed leaned forward and vomited on the leaves.

'Eeew.' Dylan sounded disgusted.

I glared at her. 'It's okay, Ed,' I whispered. 'It's over.'

He was shaking uncontrollably now, his breath coming out in ragged gasps.

'We need to keep moving.' Nico knelt on Ed's other side. 'Can you walk?'

Ed nodded, then he sat back on his heels and blew out his breath, clearly trying to calm himself.

'Sorry.' He turned to me, his face burning with humiliation. 'Sorry I was sick.'

'Don't be silly.' I rubbed his back again.

'We really need to go.' Nico hauled Ed to his feet.

Ed took a couple of deep breaths.

'Foster is heading this way,' Dylan announced from the trees at the edge of the wood.

'Come on.' Nico grabbed Ed's arm and led him deeper into the wood. As we walked, Ed's shaking subsided. Some colour returned to his face. We came out onto the main road. A bus was pulling up at a nearby stop.

'We should get on that,' Dylan said. 'Just to get away from here.'

'Yeah,' Nico agreed. 'Get away then work out what to do next.'

I glanced at Ed. He was walking properly now. Almost back to normal, except for the dark rings under his eyes and the haunted look inside them.

We leaped on board and made our way upstairs. The bus was fairly empty, just another group of teenagers playing music loudly at the back. I pushed Ed into the front seat and sat beside him. Nico and Dylan slid into the seat behind.

No one spoke for a moment, then I leaned over and rubbed Ed's arm.

'I'm sorry,' I said. 'I know this is difficult but can you tell us what happened? Did you find out where Lex is?'

'What about the Rainbow bomb?' Dylan added.

'It was hard.' Ed hesitated. 'He fought me. Foster. Every step of the way . . .'

I stared at him. 'What d'you mean?'

'Well, normally when I go into people's heads they can't . . . they don't seem to be able to stop me. I mean, I *can* hold myself back . . . simply look at the thoughts they want me to see . . . but if I *want* to, I can get into any part of their mind that I like.' He shivered.

'So how was it different with Foster?' I asked.

Ed swallowed. 'He tried to block me. I mean I got through some of it, but it was like . . . like . . . well, think of the hardest thing you can imagine doing, mentally, like maybe trying to remember some complicated sequence of numbers while someone's shouting a load of other numbers in your ear . . . it was like that. I had to concentrate so hard to see anything it was making me feel ill and then . . . and then . . .' his mouth wobbled, 'I felt him remembering being beaten as a child, by his dad, I think, and this other boy, his brother, was screaming at the dad to stop but the dad was out of control and he was whacking Foster around the head with his fists and all I could feel was Foster being terrified . . .' He stopped, clutching his stomach again.

I glanced at Nico and Dylan. They both looked shocked.

185

With a jolt I realised that their abilities were entirely on the outside, purely physical. They had no idea about what Ed and I went through when we saw something in our heads.

'That sounds horrible,' I said, gently. 'What happened next?'

'Once he knew I could feel that memory, he went berserk. I mean, inside his head he was screaming and yelling at me. The worst things I've ever heard in my life. How he was going to kill me . . . torture me . . .' Ed let out a shaky breath. 'And I tried pushing past it to find out what he knew about Lex and the Rainbow bomb, but all I could see was this one thought. He was trying to hide it but it was too strong. *It's Rick.* He kept thinking it over and over. *Rick. Rick.*'

'Who's Rick?' Dylan asked.

'Foster's brother – the one he wants released from jail,' Ed said.

'And the reason why Foster stole the bomb and is doing all this,' I added.

'So after a bit I managed to see a few more things and then Foster blocked everything again,' Ed went on, 'and all I could hear was what he would do to me once I wasn't holding him inside his head any more. And that's when I realised . . . it wasn't just me holding him . . . *He* was holding *me* too . . . trapping me . . . stopping me from controlling the connection. And I panicked. That's never happened to me before. I've always been able to break the connection whenever I wanted . . .'

'And you did in the end,' I reminded him. 'You *did* break away.'

Ed nodded.

'So did you see where Ketty's brother is being kept?' Nico asked.

Ed nodded again. My heart leaped.

'An empty building in King's Cross. Up from the station on the right side. Near the canal. I didn't get an exact address but there's a pub next door that Foster couldn't hide the name of – the Dog and Duck.'

'And what about the Rainbow bomb?' Dylan insisted.

'No.' Ed shook his head. 'Foster was blocking that *really* hard. I've got no idea.'

Dylan sat back, clearly frustrated.

I peered outside the bus window, my heart racing. We were approaching Hampstead tube. It was only a few stops from here down to King's Cross. I stood up.

'I'm going after Lex,' I said.

'No.' Nico stood up too, his expression fierce. '*We're* going after Lex,' he said. '*All* of us, right?' He looked at Ed.

'Of course.' Ed struggled to his feet.

'All for one . . .' Dylan drawled sarcastically. But she stood up too.

I gazed round at them. 'You don't have—'

'Will you get off the freakin' bus, Ketty.' Nico rolled his eyes. '*Move.*'

We walked out of King's Cross station and headed up York Way, the road to the right of the main terminal. A million thoughts swirled inside my head. Once we found the building, how were we going to get Lex out? Would anyone else be there, like guards, or Foster himself? I was worried for Lex and for the other three, especially Ed. He was walking on ahead, hands shoved in his pockets. Foster's memories must have been really bad to have made him actually vomit.

We moved into single file as we passed under some scaffolding. I caught up with Dylan as we re-emerged. I'd completely lost track of time, but it was dark now . . . the street lamps casting gloomy shadows across our path.

'D'you think Ed's okay?' I said.

Dylan glanced at him. 'No, but he will be.' She sighed. 'He's tougher than you think.'

I wasn't sure that was true, but I let it slide.

'Thanks for doing this,' I said.

Dylan shot me a sideways look. 'He's your brother,' she said, as if that explained everything.

It struck me how little I knew about her.

'Do you have one?' I asked, feeling slightly awkward. 'A brother, I mean?'

Dylan shook her head. 'I've got two cousins in America. Paige is totally toxic, but Tod . . . we weren't real close but I get on with him better than anyone else in my family . . . he's five years older than me.'

'Just like me and Lex.'

Dylan nodded. 'Not that I'd do all this for Tod.' She paused. 'There's nobody I'd do this for.'

We walked on. Ed was pointing at some buildings up ahead. I guessed we must be close. My stomach twisted over.

I looked at Dylan again. Her perfectly oval face was lit by the street lamp we were passing. 'But you *are* doing this – helping, I mean . . .' I hesitated. 'You're doing this for *us*. For the four of us . . . aren't you?'

For a second a look of vulnerability flickered across Dylan's face, then her expression grew hard and still.

'Don't flatter yourself,' she snarled. 'There just wasn't anything good to watch on TV tonight.'

'Dylan? Ketty?' Nico beckoned us forward. He indicated the pub at the end of the row of houses ahead. 'The Dog and Duck. Ed reckons the place Lex is being kept is two doors down – the one with the blue door.'

Forgetting Dylan, I studied the house. It was a terrace on three storeys with a separate basement entrance. Ed pointed down to a hefty front door at the bottom of a short flight of iron steps. 'He's in there.'

'Okay, here's the plan,' Nico said. 'Dylan and I break in and find Lex. Ed and Ketty stay outside by the basement front door, ready to call us if anyone approaches.'

'What? Why do I have to wait outside?' I complained.

'Because it could be dangerous . . . we don't know who else is in there apart from Lex.'

'But I can help. I can look after my—'

'Not if you have a vision,' Dylan said. 'Who's going to look after you if you go into one of those weird trances of yours.'

I stared at her.

'She's right, Ketty.' Nico touched my cheek. 'We'll all be safer if you wait outside.'

189

I bit my lip. 'Okay,' I agreed.

We crept down the iron stairs. The basement looked deserted. The only room visible from outside was dark and empty. A single light bulb hung from the ceiling. Nico examined the bars on the window.

'No way of getting through them.' He turned his attention to the door, running his hands down the side. 'A Chubb and two Yales.' He stood back, focusing on the locks. 'We'll be okay so long as there isn't a London bar reinforcing the door frame.'

I glanced back up to the street as Nico worked on each lock in turn. Ed paced up and down.

The first lock clicked open. My heart thumped. The second and third followed. Nico grabbed the handle of the door and pushed. It swung open into silence.

'Come on.' He beckoned Dylan.

They disappeared inside.

I waited, my throat dry. Seconds later they were back.

'He's not there,' Dylan said.

'But we found some rope and a tray with old food on it,' Nico added.

'And we found this.' Dylan held up a faded jacket. 'Do you recognise it?'

'Yes.' It was the jacket Lex had been wearing at the Rufus Stone and in Highgate Cemetery. My throat tightened. 'It's his.'

Nico shook his head. 'I'm sorry, Ketts.' He put his arm round my shoulders. 'Foster must have got here before we did. Taken him away.' He hugged me. 'It doesn't mean anything. Lex could still be okay.'

I shook my head as the full weight of the discovery pressed down on me. The plan hadn't worked. We hadn't been able to move fast enough. And, worst of all, Foster knew I'd tried to trick him. He was angry. Maybe angry enough to kill Lex in revenge. My heart pounded again, the fear overwhelming me

I pressed my face into Lex's jacket, sniffing in his smell of motorbike oil and woody aftershave. *I need to see Lex*, I said to myself. *I need to see where he is.* I squeezed my eyes shut tighter. Please *let me see.*

Without warning, in a single flash of light, the vision erupted in front of my eyes.

I'm back in the dark corridor, panting for breath. There's the door. I push it open. There he is. Lex. Gagged. Chained to a radiator. Terrified. I pull off the gag. Stare at his face. I know there's something I have to ask him.' What's the day,' I say. 'What?' Lex's eyes are wild. 'Listen, Ket—'

'Tell me the day and time.' I say. I look round. There's a stool in the corner. A piano. I know this room. Lex frowns. 'It's Thursday, late evening . . . I've got no idea what time . . . Listen, there's a bomb—' 'I know. Where's Foster?' I say. 'He wasn't here. Soames brought me here. Listen, Ketty. There's a bomb.'

I jerked out of the vision, but not into full consciousness. Like a drowning swimmer clawing for the surface, I gasped for breath.

'Oh no, oh no, oh no.' I could hear my voice moaning but it sounded like it was coming from far away. 'Is it Thursday . . . Thursday?'

Nico was holding me up, his voice muffled and frantic. 'Ketty? Ketty?'

'What's happened to her?' Ed in the distance.

'Give her some air.' Dylan's voice sounded closer.

I snapped out of it, taking my own weight, heaving myself up, out of Nico's arms. 'Is it Thursday?' I demanded.

'Yes, Ketty, *Jesus*,' Nico shook my shoulders. I could feel his fear radiating through my whole body. 'What the hell happened?'

'I brought on a vision,' I said, still panting. 'I made myself see him . . . Lex . . . where he'll be later tonight.'

'Wow.' Nico's eyes widened.

'He was chained up,' I went on. 'He couldn't get away. He was trying to tell me about the Rainbow bomb.'

Silence. The others stared at me.

'So where's he going to be tonight?' Dylan asked.

I blinked, pulling fully away from Nico. I looked round at them all, still hardly able to believe what I'd seen.

'The music room in the basement at Fox Academy.'

22: Finding Lex

'Your brother is being taken to our *school*?' Nico stared at me. 'How's Foster going to get him there?'

'And why?' Dylan put her hands on her hips.

'Foster isn't taking Lex himself,' I said. 'Soames is.'

'Who?' Ed asked.

I swallowed, my heart still racing. Soames was the man Foster had telephoned while we were at Highgate Cemetery . . . the man Foster had ordered to find the others after they'd taken the flash drive from the office car park hut.

Shoot the little bastards on sight . . . Foster's order echoed in my ears.

'Soames works for Foster.' I looked at Nico. 'He's dangerous. Violent. We have to get back to school before he arrives with Lex.'

'But why would he take Lex to our school?' Dylan persisted.

Ignoring her, Ed's eyes widened. 'Suppose they're already there? Someone at school might have been hurt.'

'I don't think so,' I said. 'In the vision, Lex said it was late evening.'

'But they could be on their way.' Nico's face blanched. I knew he was thinking about his stepdad. 'Suppose Lex makes a noise and somebody at school sees them? Soames might lash out and—'

'No.' I shook my head. 'I've *seen* Lex. He's going to be chained up and, anyway, the music room's soundproofed. You can get in by that fire door at the top of the stairs. No-one's ever there in the evenings.'

'Why don't we phone Geri?' Ed rubbed his forehead. 'If Lex is there, she can go down and get him. If he hasn't arrived yet, she can evacuate the school and keep a lookout for him and Soames.'

'Yes.' Nico nodded. 'Maybe Soames will know where Foster and the Rainbow bomb are too.'

I hesitated. Geri still thought Lex was hiding out in France. Telling her he was Foster's prisoner would mean revealing I had lied to her. On the other hand, it sounded like Soames was going to leave Lex on his own – which meant he was safe. And Foster was still in possession of the Rainbow bomb. Maybe Soames really *did* know where it was going to go off.

'I still don't see why Foster would order Lex to be taken to our school and chained up in a music room,' Dylan said.

Nico pulled out his phone. He handed it to me.

'Call Geri,' he said. 'That emergency number she gave us is programmed in under her name.'

I looked at him. There wasn't any choice.

Geri answered after three rings. 'What's wrong, dear?' She sounded distracted.

'I've had another vision,' I explained. 'I know where my brother is.'

'I thought he was with friends in France?'

'Er . . . no . . . I've . . . er . . . Foster has kidnapped him,' I said.

'You saw this in a vision?' Geri didn't sound convinced. 'Do you think this one is more reliable than your precognition over the hospitals?'

Oh, God. My head swam, remembering the way I'd lied to Geri before. I closed my eyes. There was only one way through this. One way to make sure Lex was safe.

This time, I was going to have to tell her the whole truth.

'No . . .' I said, slowly, opening my eyes again. 'Foster kidnapped Lex yesterday, *before* I told you about the visions. He did it to blackmail me . . . he . . . he made me lie about the bombs at the two hospitals.'

There was a tense silence.

'You mean you *made up* a vision? *Two* visions?' Geri spluttered. 'You knew from the start there was no bomb at Linhurst Hospital? That the real target was Gayton? That your brother *wasn't* in France?'

'Yes . . .' I hesitated.

'Why didn't you tell me, for God's sake?'

'Because of Lex . . . Foster said he was going to kill Lex if I didn't do what he said.'

195

'So your response to this was to *lie* to me?' Geri sucked in her breath. 'D'you have any idea how much manpower was invested in attempting to protect Linhurst Hospital – all based on *my* recommendations following *your* supposed insights? Not to mention the waste of resources in getting Interpol to try and track down your brother?'

'Yes, I'm sorry.' My heart was sinking. 'But . . . but it proves my visions do work. And this latest one . . . it shows where my brother is. He's at our school and—'

'Foster knows where you go to school?' Geri snapped. 'How?'

'I'm not sure,' I said. 'But he'd heard about Medusa already, so—'

'He knows about the Medusa Project as well?'

'He doesn't know much,' I said, trying to reassure her. 'He was asking me questions.'

'And you still didn't think to tell me any of this?' Geri's voice burned with rage.

'No, and I'm sorry, but the thing is, Foster is taking Lex to our school now and—'

'Foster is on his way to Fox Academy?' Geri sounded doubtful.

'No,' I admitted. 'He . . . he isn't taking Lex himself. He's making this man called Soames take him. We . . . I was with Foster earlier and—'

'You *met* with Foster this evening? Where? When?' Geri now sounded incredulous.

'We saw him in Hampstead Heath about an hour ago.'

196

'*We* . . . you mean you're with Nico and Ed and Dylan?' Geri's voice rose to a shriek. 'And *none* of you had the sense to tell me *anything* about *any* of this?'

Oh shit, oh shit. Now I'd got everyone else into trouble as well. 'I was trying to protect my brother. The others were just helping. Please don't be cross with them.'

I stared helplessly round at the others. Ed was staring at the pavement. Nico offered me a sympathetic smile. Dylan rolled her eyes.

'Ketty, I am beyond disappointed in you,' Geri snapped. 'And all this will have to be dealt with, but right now I'm nowhere near your school. We've had a solid lead on Foster *and* the Rainbow bomb. We told Foster earlier we weren't going to release his brother and he's responded by announcing that the Rainbow bomb will go off this evening in a central London location. Because of my initial involvement through you, the powers that be want me at our HQ, near to where we're expecting Foster.'

'But what about Lex?' I insisted.

'When does what you saw in the vision happen?' Geri snapped.

'I don't know,' I said. 'Sometime this evening.'

'I'll have an agent sent over to keep an eye out for this man – Soames – who you say you saw in your vision,' Geri went on.

'I didn't actually see Soames,' I said, trying to explain. 'Lex just said Soames had brought him to the school and chained him in the music room in the basement.'

'Why would Foster divert manpower to something so

pointless?' Geri's sceptical tone echoed Dylan's earlier. 'Look, you said yourself you don't know when this vision happens. It all sounds a bit hazy.'

'It isn't,' I insisted.

Geri cleared her throat. 'Where are you?'

'Near King's Cross station.'

'Well, get back to school straight away. I'll call ahead and explain to Fergus what you've seen – tell him my agent is on his way. We'll talk later.' Geri hung up.

I turned to the others. 'She's sending some agent to the school but I'm not sure she even believes Lex will be there.'

'It does seem kinda weird.' Dylan wrinkled her nose.

Nico took his phone back. 'I'm calling Fergus.' We walked to King's Cross tube while Nico had a brief conversation with his stepdad. We could all hear Mr Fox ranting on the other end. My heart sank still further. Nico and the others were going to be in so much trouble and it was all my fault.

Nico ended the call. 'Well, that was fun,' he said.

'What did he say about Lex?' I asked.

'He was so angry he hardly even listened, but once Geri's agent arrives he's going to take him to check the basement music room.'

'Just him and the agent?' I asked. 'Supposing Soames is lying in wait for him?'

'Why would Foster have Soames *do* that?' Dylan butted in. 'I think you're losing perspective, Ketty. Foster wants to send a message to the British Government, not to the head teacher of a boarding school.'

'But it's *our* school,' I went on.

Ed cleared his throat. 'Maybe that's why Foster has had Lex taken there. To show he knows where we're based. To unnerve everyone.'

This was the first thing anyone had said that made sense. I kept going over it as we went into King's Cross station and got on a train.

Mr Fox met us at the other end. He was clearly livid, his face almost purple with rage.

'How *dare* you leave school without permission?' he roared. 'How *dare* you meet a known criminal without even *telling* me or Geri that he had contacted you? I've stuck my neck out for you four over these missions she's making you do and instead of thanking me you go off on your own, putting your lives at even *greater* risk. It's *completely* unacceptable behaviour.'

I hung my head. It was one thing Geri being cross, but I hated upsetting Mr Fox – he'd always tried to look out for me . . . for us.

'I'm sorry.' I looked up, feeling guilty now, as well as hugely anxious about Lex. 'Did you go down to the basement music room?'

'Yes,' Mr Fox snapped. 'There's no sign of your brother, but all external doors have been double locked and the agent Geri sent over is keeping guard near the front door.'

I frowned, wishing I knew when Lex and Soames were arriving.

Five minutes later and we were back at school. The place was quiet – 9.30 p.m. was the curfew for getting back on a school night – and all the students were either in the common rooms or their dorms.

'I thought you said the agent Geri sent was at the front of the school?' Nico said as we entered the main hall.

Mr Fox looked round, perplexed.

'Maybe he heard something and went to investigate,' I said.

'*Look!*' Ed pointed to the reception room door to the left of the big fireplace.

A body lay in the doorway. It was James, the agent who'd been with Maria when she'd driven us to the Fostergames office car park.

Mr Fox knelt down and felt the man's pulse. 'He's alive, but unconscious. Stay put, I'm calling for help.' He went inside the reception room.

'This means Soames must be here.' I glanced at the others. 'I have to get down to the music room. Find Lex.'

'But Soames could still be with him.' Ed blanched.

'I can deal with Soames.' Nico took my hand. 'Come on.'

We raced along the corridor. Down the steps towards the canteen then left towards the science block. As we descended to the basement I glanced over my shoulder. Dylan and Ed were right behind us.

I jumped the last few steps and flew along the corridor. It was dark, just like in my vision. No time to waste switching on the light. My pulse raced. This was it. We were nearly there.

Down some more stairs. A right turn. A left.

I stopped, panting, in front of the music room door. Nico skidded to a stop beside me. He braced himself. I pushed open the door.

Lex was alone. He stood on the other side of the room, a scarf round his mouth, his left wrist chained to a radiator. I ran over, my heart pounding. He looked terrified, his eyes wild. As soon as he saw me, he mumbled something behind his gag. I yanked at the scarf, desperate to free his mouth. As I pulled the binding away I remembered what I needed to ask.

'What's the day?'

'What?' Lex's eyes were wild and unfocused. 'Listen, Ket—'

'Tell me the day and time.' Weird though it was, I knew I had to make him say it so it would be in the vision I'd already had. I reminded myself to look round the room so I would recognise it in the vision too. There was the piano stool. There was the piano.

Lex frowned. 'It's Thursday, late evening . . . I've got no idea what time . . . Listen, there's a bomb—'

'I know. Where's Foster?'

Lex glanced at the others, then back to me. 'He wasn't here. Soames brought me here. Listen, Ketty. There's a bomb.'

God, he looked so scared.

'We know there's a bomb. Geri's onto it.' Nico picked up the chain attached to Lex's wrist. 'This is going to need bolt cutters.'

My eyes filled with tears of relief. I had found him. It was over. Whatever Foster did now, Lex was safe.

'D'you know exactly where the bomb is?' Dylan asked.

'Yes.' Lex grabbed my arm with his free hand. 'Listen, Ketty, you have to get everyone out of here. Now.'

'What?' I frowned. 'Why?'

'It's the bomb.' Lex let go of my arm and lifted his jumper. A slim black box was strapped to his shirt.

I stared at it. Beside me, Ed gasped.

'This is the Rainbow bomb,' Lex said. 'And it's programmed to explode in eight minutes.'

23: Countdown

The Rainbow bomb was sleek and black – the size of a pocket laptop. I stared at its smooth casing, taped tightly round Lex's shirt. My heart pounded.

'Well, let's just take it off you.' Nico reached out to unstrap the bomb.

'No.' Lex backed away. 'There's a trigger attached to the bomb. When Foster put this on me he explained that if anyone tried to take it off, the trigger would be released and the bomb would detonate immediately.'

'Then how do we stop it?' My guts were in free fall, a terrible tight feeling across my chest.

'We have to call Geri. Get her to send bomb disposal,' Nico said.

'There's no time,' Lex said. 'I saw the timer when Foster set the bomb. It's below a panel on the underneath bit.' He pointed to the bottom of the device. 'I reckon there's only a few minutes to go.'

'No.' My head was spinning. This couldn't be happening.

Ed bent down and examined the panel.

'Ketty, please leave,' Lex pleaded. 'You have to save yourselves and there are other people here too – kids and teachers. They'll be hurt when it goes off. You have to warn them.'

'It's not going to go off,' I said.

'We still have to tell Fergus,' Nico said, his voice full of concern. 'He can get everyone out . . . evacuate the school . . .'

Dylan nodded. 'Go.'

Nico sped off.

'Why is Foster doing this?' I stared at Lex's strained face. I couldn't believe what was happening. I *couldn't* lose him.

'It's his revenge for the government not releasing his brother,' Lex said. 'And on me for trying to sell him out to a journalist, I guess.' He smiled. 'Please go now, Ketty. This won't be so bad as long as I know you're safe.'

'No.' My eyes filled with tears. 'No, I'm not leaving.'

'There must be something we can try,' Dylan insisted. 'Some way of defusing the bomb. We've got enough powers between us . . . maybe you or Ed . . .?'

I turned my face to the overhead panel light, blinking to bring on a vision. Perhaps if I focused hard enough I could find out what was going to happen. Work out what we needed to do.

Flashing lights . . . a sweet, heavy smell . . .

BOOM . . . a massive explosion . . . I'm turning . . . watching from a distance . . . Fox Academy in flames . . . smoke pouring up, into the sky . . .

I snapped out of the vision. *Oh my God.* I froze. The bomb was going to go off.

I'd seen it.

'What?' Dylan grabbed my arm. 'What did you see?'

'Nothing.' I gritted my teeth. My heart might be dying but I wasn't going to give up. I didn't care what Ed had said before about alternate realities not existing. I wouldn't believe everything was all mapped out in front of me.

This was a future I *had* to change.

'What about your ability, Dylan?' I said. 'Could you use your defence powers to protect Lex from the blast? You know, get between him and the blast somehow . . . lessen its impact?'

She shook her head. 'I could maybe resist some of the fallout – pieces of brick or whatever, but the force of the actual bomb would be way bigger than anything I've managed to protect myself from so far.'

I turned to Ed. 'How about if you mind-read Lex?'

Ed was still examining the panel on the underside of the bomb. He glanced up at me. 'That won't help unless Lex knows how to defuse the bomb.'

'Which I don't,' Lex added. 'You have to get out of here, Ketty.'

Ignoring him, I tried to focus. 'What about the wires, Ed?' I said, remembering the conversation we'd had before we went to the hospital. 'Didn't you tell me something about coloured wires?'

'I think the wires are under this panel.' Ed glanced up at us. 'Shall I try taking it off?'

'Yes.'

'When Ketty's left the room,' Lex said.

'I'm not going any—'

'For God's sake, get on with it,' Dylan snapped.

A tense silence. Ed eased off the panel at the base of the bomb. Together we bent down and examined what was underneath.

Seven coloured wires were strung along the underside of the bomb. Beside them was a small keypad. Above that, the timer – the numbers displayed in red – was counting down in minutes and seconds.

04.45

04.44

04.43

Oh, God.

Ed bit his lip.

'What does it say?' Dylan asked.

I looked up. 'We've got about four and a half minutes.'

'It'll be a big explosion,' Lex added, his voice shaking. 'Bring down half the school. That's why you all need to leave now.'

'No.'

'*Please*, Ketty. If I could walk away from you I would.' Lex held up his wrist, still chained to the radiator. 'But I can't, so you *have* to walk away from me.'

'No.' My eyes filled with tears. I turned to Ed. 'Didn't you tell me you have to cut the wires in a specific order?'

'Yes.' Ed rubbed his forehead. 'The order of the colours of the rainbow. Red then orange then yellow then . . .'

206

'I'll do it,' I said. 'I'll cut the wires.'

Ed stared at me. 'But suppose the bomb goes off while you're doing it? Suppose just cutting the wires isn't enough?'

'It's going to go off anyway,' Dylan said. 'Ketty's right. We have to try.'

'You *can't*, Ketty. *Please*.' Lex's own eyes were filling up now, his whole body trembling. 'Think of Mum and Dad . . . they can't lose *both* of us.'

I looked round the room. There was nothing to cut the wires with in here.

'We need pliers,' Dylan said.

I checked the timer. 04.21 . . . 04.20 . . . 04.19 . . .

I met Dylan's eye and the same idea hit both of us at the same instant.

'The tech room,' she said.

'Come on.'

We raced through the dark corridor. Nico was flying down the stairs towards us as we reached the first set of steps.

'Fergus is evacuating the school,' he said. 'He told me to make you go upstairs now.'

'You go,' I said to Dylan. 'Nico can get Ed. I'll handle the wires on my own.' I pushed past them and up the steps.

I could hear them talking behind me. Then footsteps. I glanced round. Dylan was chasing after me. I didn't say anything as we raced along the ground floor. The fire alarm suddenly screeched out. A loud voice yelled over the top of it.

'Uncle Fergus,' Dylan said.

We could hear him in the distance. 'Hurry to the Top Field. Now. *Hurry*.'

We ran past the science labs and burst, panting, through the art room door. I raced across to the tech room.

'How much time d'you think we have?' I said.

Dylan shook her head. 'Under three minutes.'

I looked round, frantic.

'There.' A row of pliers was ranged inside a glass cabinet that stood against the far wall.

I raced over. The door was locked.

'Oh *shit*.' I looked round for a key, panic filling my head.

Smash. Dylan's fist broke the glass door. She yanked out a pair of pliers. I stared at her hand. Not a scratch.

'Come on.' She turned and raced back.

The corridors were full of people now. Sleepy younger kids trailing dressing gowns and older ones giggling excitedly. They had no idea what was about to happen.

'Hurry,' I kept saying as we pushed past them. 'Get out of the building.'

We pelted down the first set of stairs. As we ran along the dark corridor below I had a sudden sense of déjà vu from one of my first visions when I'd seen myself running and running. Foster's voice had been in my head. *Rick*, he'd said. *It's all about Rick.*

Down the second set of stairs. How much time was left?

We ran, panting, back into the music room. Lex was leaning against the wall, his face drained of colour. Nico was beside him, Ed kneeling, still examining the Rainbow wires.

'Ketty, *please* go,' Lex pleaded.

'Everybody else should leave,' I said. 'I'm staying.' I took the pliers from Dylan and knelt beside Ed. I glanced at the timer.

02.36 . . . 02.35 . . . 02.34 . . .

Oh God. I shook myself. *Focus.* There were the wires.

'Just tell me what the order is,' I said to Ed. 'Then you all have to go.'

Ed cleared his throat. 'Er . . . red, orange, yellow, green, blue . . .'

'I'm sure it's blue before green,' Nico insisted.

'No.' Ed shook his head. 'Green, blue, indigo, violet.'

I stared at the wires. The first four were obvious. But what was the difference between blue and indigo and violet?

'Blue before green,' Nico repeated.

'Richard of York gave battle in vain,' Ed said stubbornly, standing up. 'Red, orange, yellow, green, blue, indigo, violet.'

I touched the three wires I wasn't sure about. My fingers trembled. 'Which is which?'

Dylan knelt beside me. She pointed at the brightest blue wire. 'Blue,' she said firmly. She pointed at the darkest wire – it was almost black . . . an inky blue. 'Indigo,' she said.

I nodded, gratefully, then pointed to the bluey-purple wire myself. 'Violet.'

'You got it.' Dylan stood up. 'Go.'

I held the pliers over the red wire. The timer passed two minutes.

01.59 seconds . . . 01.58 . . . 01.57 . . .

My hands were shaking too much to hold the pliers steady.

'Here.' Nico took them from me. 'I'll do it.'

'But you three should *go*.' My words came out almost as sobs.

'All *four* of you should go.' Tears were streaming down Lex's face.

'I'm not leaving you,' I said.

'And I'm not leaving Ketty.' Nico held the pliers over the red wire.

'Neither am I,' said Ed.

Lex looked at Dylan.

'Guess we're all staying, then,' she said, her voice tight with tension.

I held Lex's hand. 'It's okay,' I said. 'It's going to be okay.' I looked down at the timer.

01.39 . . . 01.38 . . . 01.37 . . .

'Do it, Nico,' I said.

He took a deep breath, whispered something to himself that sounded like a prayer – and cut into the red wire.

24: The password

The seconds ticked away.

01.35 . . . 01.34 . . . 01.33 . . .

Silence. The tension was unbearable. Everyone held their breath as Nico snipped the red wire in half. He paused.

'I think that worked,' he said shakily.

'Keep going,' I urged.

01.30 . . . 01.29 . . . 01.28 . . . Nico cut the orange wire. Then the yellow.

He glanced round at Ed.

'Green,' he said firmly.

01.22 . . . 01.21 . . . 01.20 . . .

Nico cut the green wire. 'Oh, man.'

Lex's whole body was trembling, the sweat pouring off his forehead.

Nico opened the pliers. His hands were shaking horribly.

'Now blue,' ordered Dylan.

01.15 . . . 01.14 . . . 01.13 . . .

Nico tried to hold the pliers steady but his hands were trembling too much. 'Shit,' he muttered.

'My turn,' I said, firmly. I took the pliers and held them over the blue wire. I took a deep breath. *Come on.* Snip.

'Now the indigo.' Dylan pointed.

Cut.

01.03 . . . 01.02 . . . 01.01

I held the pliers over the final, violet wire. 'This is it.'

I cut down hard.

There was a moment's silence, then Ed let out a strangled moan.

'Oh, no,' he gasped.

'What?' Dylan shrieked.

'It's still counting down.'

'WHAT!' Lex shouted.

I checked. Ed was right. The seconds were flashing away. Less than a minute to go.

52 . . . 51 . . .

'How?' Nico clutched his head. '*Shit. SHIT!*'

'Look.' I pointed to the keypad under the timer. The four asterisks in the screen were flashing.

'There must be a code,' Dylan said. 'Four numbers.'

'Or four letters.' Ed frowned. 'A word . . . a password . . .'

42 . . . 41 . . .

Panic swirled in my head.

'Get out!' Lex yelled.

Nico swore. 'How can we work out a freakin' password in thirty seconds?'

212

'It's got to be something that matters to Foster,' Ed cried.
33 . . . 32 . . .

'How the hell can we know that?' Dylan shrieked.

'A birth date . . .' Ed said desperately. 'An anniversary . . .
a name . . .'

A name. I looked across at Nico. He was staring, eyes
wide, at the timer.

24 . . . 23 . . .

My heart pounded. I was going to lose him and my own
life – and Lex.

I looked up at my brother. His eyes were fixed on me – full
of fear and longing and love.

'Go, Ketty,' he said. 'Please.'

My heart thudded faster than the seconds still ticking
away.

19 . . . 18 . . .

Dylan reached out to the keypad. 'We have to try something,' she said. 'Anything.'

'Oh, shit,' Nico breathed.

'Please go.' Lex was still staring at me. 'Please, it's all
about *you*, Ketty.'

14 . . . 13 . . .

All about you. Foster's words echoed in my head: *All
about Rick.*

Dylan's hand hovered over the keypad. She pointed her
forefinger, ready to press a random key.

11 . . . 10 . . .

'Stop!' I said.

Dylan froze. The whole room shrank to the tiny keypad.

'It's Foster's brother,' I said. 'That's why he's doing this.'

The others stared at me.

'It's Rick,' I said. 'The password is Rick.'

7 . . . 6 . . .

Fingers shaking I tapped in the letters.

R . . .

5

I . . .

4

C . . .

3

K . . .

2

I held my breath.

The timer stopped, the number '2' flashing away.

For a second we all stood in complete shock and silence then the room erupted in yells and cheers, just as the bomb disposal team raced in.

An hour later and the four of us were gathered in Mr Fox's office. Nico and I were sitting on the desk. Nico's arm was draped round my shoulder. Dylan was sprawled over Mr Fox's armchair while Ed stood with his back to us, staring out of the window.

We were waiting for Mr Fox and Geri Paterson and had been told on pain of various torments not to move. I wanted to see Lex. After the bomb disposal people had removed his chains, he'd been taken away to have the defused bomb unstrapped from his chest. I wondered how he was and how soon I'd be able to see him.

'What's out the window, Ed?' Nico asked, lazily teleporting the ornaments on Mr Fox's desk in the air in a circle.

'Not much,' Ed admitted. 'Kids leaving the school . . . an ambulance . . .'

'An ambulance?' I was off the desk and at the window in a few seconds. It was dark outside, the only light was coming from the office we were sitting in. In the distance people from our class were hurrying towards the front gate. I watched Billy and Lola dawdling at the back, their arms round each other. Mr Rogerson went over, clearly telling them to speed up. They disappeared through the school gates.

No sign of an ambulance there. I peered into the shadows nearer the window.

There. Hidden from the students by a brick wall, a van with a red cross on the side was parked close to the fire door that led down to the basement music room. As I watched, two men I didn't recognise came through the fire door. They were pushing a hospital trolley topped with a stretcher and covered with a sheet. There was clearly a body underneath the sheet. It moved slightly as the trolley rattled and bumped its way towards the van.

My throat tightened. Was that Lex?

'Why is there an ambulance?' I said. 'D'you think there was a problem with the bomb?'

The trolley reached the van. The two men opened the van

215

doors and slid the covered stretcher into the back. The vision I'd had earlier – of the school in flames – leaped into my head.

For the past hour I'd firmly believed that I'd changed the future and stopped that explosion from ever happening. Now, suddenly, doubt crept into my mind.

How could I know what I'd seen?

How could I know what I'd changed?

Maybe the bomb was still going to go off.

'I don't see how there could have been a problem.' Nico joined us at the window. 'We'd have heard an explosion.'

'Yeah, and we didn't,' Dylan drawled from her armchair. 'No loud bangs . . . no body parts in the playground . . .'

I stared at the van as the two men closed the back doors. My heart raced.

'I have to find out if Lex is okay,' I said, running for the door.

I reached it just as Geri and Fergus arrived. I collided with Geri.

Wham.

'Sit.' She gripped my arm. 'You have a lot of explaining to do, young lady.'

'But I want to see my brother—'

'Lex is being dealt with.'

My heart seemed to stop beating. '*Dealt* with?'

Nico was suddenly by my side, his arm round my shoulder again. 'What does that mean?' he said.

'Sit.' Geri pushed me towards one of the three spare chairs

in front of the desk. I sat, with Nico and Ed on either side. Dylan perched on the arm of her much larger chair.

Mr Fox stood beside Geri. Even in my traumatised state, worrying about Lex, I had time to clock that he looked livid with rage.

God, they were both absolutely furious with me.

'Ketty's brother Lex has been taken to a safe location,' Geri said, her voice clipped. 'Only the squad who discovered him and the people in this room know that he is alive. We intend to keep it that way.'

I stared at her. 'What do you mean?'

'Your brother has been given false travelling papers and is being sent abroad to join your parents. Our hope is that if Foster believes he is dead, he will not bother to track him. Lex is of no interest to Foster other than as a pawn to manipulate us . . .' Geri turned her stony gaze on me. 'And, of course, *you*, Ketty.'

Everyone looked at me.

'You're sending Lex out of the country?' I said, faintly.

'But how are you going to convince Foster that he's dead?' Ed leaned forwards in his chair, his eyes not quite meeting Geri's. 'The bomb didn't go off.'

A short pause. Then Geri pursed her lips together. 'You're right that it didn't go off, Ed,' she said. 'But it will very soon.'

'But we defused it.' Dylan was on her feet. 'It—'

'Don't misunderstand me.' Geri raised her slim, manicured hand. 'The original bomb has been successfully neutralised but—'

'Thanks to Ed knowing about the coloured wires and Ketty working out Foster's password in about ten seconds flat,' Nico interrupted. 'Neither of which you've bothered to thank them for so far.'

'But we want Foster to *believe* he was successful,' Geri went on, ignoring Nico. 'We want Foster to think that while you may have managed to delay the Rainbow bomb, it *has* now gone off. The bomb, remember, is Foster's revenge against the British government for refusing to release Rick. We're hoping that once he feels he's made his point he'll slip under the radar for a while, giving us a chance to track him down before he makes his next move. His company's assets are frozen and the full extent of his debts has been revealed, so there's a big paper trail for us to follow as—'

'Hang on,' Nico interrupted. 'Never mind Foster. Go back to what you were saying about the bomb. How are you going to get Foster to believe it went off this evening?'

Geri pursed her lips. 'By exploding it ourselves.'

I gasped. Next to me, Ed's mouth fell open.

'*What?*' Dylan put her hands on her hips. 'You're going to *explode* the Rainbow bomb yourself?'

'Yes.' Geri sighed. 'It won't convince Foster otherwise. The evacuation of the school is almost complete now. No one will be hurt.'

'But the school.' I stared at Mr Fox. His jaw was clenched, his eyes dark.

'Fox Academy will be destroyed,' he said. 'At least, a large part of it will be. We will have to close down until the autumn term to allow for rebuilding work.'

I glanced at Nico and Ed beside me. They looked equally shocked. Ed rubbed his forehead.

'But where's everyone going to go?' he said

'Where are *we* going to go?' Nico added.

Oh my God. This was all my fault. If I'd gone to Geri in the first place – as soon as I'd had the very first vision – all this could have been avoided.

Geri would have kept Lex safe. His meeting with Foster would never have happened. And Mr Fox wouldn't be losing his school.

'I'm so sorry,' I said.

'I don't blame *you*, Ketty.' Mr Fox glared at Geri. 'I blame the Medusa Project. I blame a covert operation that uses and manipulates children to—'

'Fergus will be given the resources to set up a temporary school in another location,' Geri snapped. She glared at Mr Fox – a cold, poisonous stare.

'So we'll be going *there*?' I asked.

'No.' Geri looked at each one of us in turn. 'It's not safe for you to be near Mr Fox right now. Foster knows you attend Fox Academy which means that, wherever the school is based, you may be targets.'

'So we have to wait until you catch Foster before we can go back to school?' Ed asked.

'It's not just Foster,' I said. 'He told me he had a contact in the security services – someone who gave him details about the Medusa Project. About us.'

Geri nodded. 'I suspected as much once I realised Foster had fooled us this afternoon,' she said. 'This isn't the first leak in the department, though it's the first one concerning Medusa. We'll investigate, but if there's really a mole, that's all the more reason to get you away from here.'

'So where are you sending us?' Dylan demanded.

'Abroad,' Geri said vaguely. 'To a training camp.'

I glanced at Nico. He was staring at Mr Fox. With a jolt I realised that taking Nico away from school wasn't like taking the rest of us. Mr Fox was his stepdad – his only family. How was that going to make him feel?

'What *sort* of training camp?' I asked.

'One that will teach you responsibility and discipline,' Geri said briskly.

'You mean a *boot* camp?' Dylan's jaw dropped.

'If you like.' Geri crossed her arms. 'I thought that keeping you based in an ordinary school, training you in basic attack and defence skills and sending you on simple missions to test your emerging powers would minimise the need for anything more sophisticated until you were older. But, as Ketty has proved, this was a mistake.'

Everyone looked at me again. I could feel my face reddening.

'*I* don't need a bloody boot camp.' Nico spoke for the first time, addressing his words to Mr Fox. 'I already have responsibility and discipline.'

Mr Fox shook his head. He stared down at the floor. 'This is not my decision,' he said in a low voice. 'I'm not being given a choice here.'

'It's only for two months,' Geri said, her voice tight.

I glanced at Ed. He was biting his lip.

'What about our psychic skills?' he said. 'What about all the training we were doing with Mr Fox?'

'Basic discipline comes first,' Geri said.

'What does *that* mean?' Nico said, angrily.

Geri shook her head. 'You'll find out.'

'So when do we go?' I said.

'Tonight,' Geri explained. 'You have ten minutes to pack a small bag, then two agents will take you to a private airport.'

The atmosphere tightened immediately.

'*Tonight?*' Dylan snarled. 'No freakin' *way.*'

'Tonight.' Geri said, in a voice that made it clear there was to be no argument. 'So I suggest you hurry with the packing. You'll only need a few spare clothes. A toothbrush . . . trainers. Everything else will be provided.'

'What about Lex?' I said, glancing outside again. There was no sign of either the trolley or the ambulance I'd seen earlier. 'Can't I even say goodbye to him?'

'I'm afraid not,' Geri said coolly. 'Lex has already left.'

I looked down at my lap, a storm of emotions whirling in my head. I shoved my hands in my pockets. Lex's troll doll was still there. I fingered the smooth plastic . . . the rough hair . . .

There was a rap at the door.

'Enter,' Geri called.

Maria and James, the male agent who we'd last seen unconscious in the reception doorway, walked in. Maria was in her usual skinny jeans and boots, though she seemed to be wearing more make-up than usual. James looked much smarter than he had before too, in a leather jacket and heavily gelled hair. They looked round the room quickly. Maria shot me a quick smile, before her eyes settled on Geri.

'We're ready,' she said.

'James and Maria will be your escorts for the journey,' Geri announced. 'Go with them now, please. And good luck.'

There was nothing else we could do. Mr Fox, Nico and Ed followed James to the boys' dorm, while Maria accompanied Dylan and me up to our own room. We packed in silence. Well, near silence. Dylan looked mutinous. She muttered under her breath as she threw clothes into her bag.

I was hardly aware of what I was taking from my drawers. It wasn't going away I minded so much, it was just all happening so fast . . . I absently found a bag and shoved in some sweats and tees and two pairs of trainers. I wished I'd had a chance to speak to Lex before he left. Still, I'd be able to write to him once he got home to Mum and Dad . . . and at least the training we were going to acquire at this boot camp place would be useful.

Dylan was still stomping about the dormitory.

'Maybe training camp won't be so bad,' I suggested as I

joined her at the large table that ran under the window. Dylan looked up from the piles of books, papers and general crap she was sifting through.

'Yeah, right,' she snorted, disentangling her mp3 player headphones from around a desk lamp. 'I was sent to a brat camp back home in the States once. It sucked big time. Cold showers. Disgusting food. Early starts. Unbelievably hard work. Demeaning chores. And that's not counting the sadistic bitches that think you're only there to carry out their orders.'

I stared at her. 'It sounds awful.'

'It's hell on earth,' Dylan said, darkly.

'Hurry up, girls,' Maria called out from the door. 'Time to leave.'

Dylan swore. 'Geri is so wrong about this,' she said. 'We're a freakin' team. We *are* disciplined already.'

I caught her arm as she turned. 'Thanks for earlier,' I said. 'I couldn't have managed the wires on that bomb without you.'

Dylan met my gaze. For a second I saw her acknowledge what I'd said – and how, for all her aggression, she appreciated my thanks. And then the familiar sneer curled across her lips. She wrinkled her nose. 'Whatever.'

Nico and Ed were waiting at the foot of the main stairs with James and Mr Fox. A large, dark-windowed 4x4 stood outside. We were bundled in, our bags placed into the boot. Mr Fox said goodbye, giving both Nico and Dylan awkward hugs and patting me and Ed on the back.

We sat in silence in the back of the car as James, with Maria next to him in the passenger seat, drove off.

The car had two rows of seats behind the drivers'. Nico and I were at the very back. In front of us, Ed and Dylan both shoved in headphones and started listening to music. Dylan's was extremely loud, but neither James nor Maria said anything.

Nico put his arm round my shoulders and I leaned against his chest. He smelled of soap powder and grass.

'I'm sorry you have to leave Mr Fox,' I said.

Nico shrugged. ''S okay.'

We were silent for a bit, lost in our own thoughts. Then Nico turned his face to mine and smiled.

'It was scary earlier,' I whispered.

He bent closer. 'I know.'

Our lips were almost touching and I felt that terrifying, overwhelming feeling again. Like he was reaching the most secret, fragile part of me.

'I'm scared now,' I whispered.

'At least we're together,' he murmured.

'I mean . . . I'm scared of . . . of how I feel . . .'

'Yeah?' Nico's lips grazed my ear. 'Me too,' he whispered. 'It's because I love you.'

We gazed at each other and, in that moment, I forgot about the past few days and boot camp and not saying good-bye to Lex and realised the truth at last.

'I love you too,' I whispered back.

Boom!

The huge explosion rocked the car. We both whipped round. Behind us, through the car window, the broken outline of Fox Academy was clearly visible. Smoke poured out of what had once been the main building, flames licked the sky.

Dylan and Ed had turned round and were staring out of the back window too. Ed's eyes were wide with horror.

'Guess they set that bomb off, then,' Dylan said drily.

I stared open-mouthed at the smoke, unable to believe my school was gone.

So my vision *had* come true. What did that mean? That I couldn't change the future after all? That, one way or another, the universe would always have its way?

We were all silent – shell-shocked – for a few minutes, then the four of us started talking – quietly, so James and Maria couldn't hear up front.

'I still don't see why Geri had to blow up the entire school,' Nico said.

'She wasn't telling the whole truth about that,' Ed said darkly. 'I could sense it.'

'Yeah, I think you're right,' Dylan agreed. 'There are loads of other ways she could have faked Lex's death.'

I sat back. Two weeks ago, I reflected, this conversation would have been impossible. Back then Nico hated Ed and Ed hated himself and everyone hated Dylan . . . but now . . . well, I guess after being in a room together when a bomb's about to kill you all, it's hard not to feel like you belong with each other.

225

Which meant Dylan was right. We were already a team.

'Team Medusa,' I murmured.

Dylan raised her eyebrows.

'What, babe?' Nico asked.

'Nothing, it's just you guys . . .' I paused, trying to work out what I wanted to say. 'It's just I've never belonged to anything, ever. Well, apart from a running club . . . And nobody ever made me feel like I belonged, either. But I do. Now. Because you three could have saved yourselves earlier but you didn't. You stayed down in that music room even though it meant risking your lives.'

Nico stared at me. 'Course we stayed,' he said.

'We're friends,' Ed said shyly.

'Plus your brother's hot,' Dylan added.

I laughed. 'Anyway, it's just that we've got to go to this horrible training camp place and I'm . . . well, I just want to say that I'm glad that . . . that you'll all be there.'

'For God's sake, babe.' Nico rolled his eyes. 'D'you think you could ratchet down the cheesiness levels a bit?'

'Yeah, because I might hurl all over Ed if you don't,' Dylan said.

Ed grinned. 'Please, Ketty,' he said. 'Think of my chinos.'

'Oh, piss off.' I laughed again.

And somehow the prospect of boot camp didn't seem quite so bad any more.

If you enjoyed *The Hostage*,
look out for the next exciting book
in THE MEDUSA PROJECT series,
The Rescue – turn the page to read
the first chapter . . .

1: Arrival

Spain was unbearably hot. We'd made a pit-stop at a roadside café after a solid five-hour drive and even though it was late afternoon, the sun was still fierce on the back of my head. Everyone else was still inside the café, but I'd come outside for a moment by myself. I was leaning against the car, the metal hot through my shirt, looking into the distance. All I could see was desert – sand . . . rocks . . . and, further away, a range of purple-tipped mountains.

The café door banged and Ketty emerged. 'Kind of bleak, isn't it, Ed?' she said, with a grimace, as she reached me. 'And way too hot to run in.'

I nodded. Ketty's my best friend – and a keen runner. Like me, she has the Medusa gene, but whereas I can read minds, Ketty can predict the future. I glanced at her, careful not to look her straight in the eye – if I make eye contact with anyone I automatically see into their thoughts and feelings.

You probably think that would be cool.

Trust me, it isn't.

Ketty looked surprisingly unbothered by the heat. She was wearing shorts and a t-shirt. No sweat patches – unlike me – though a couple of her dark brown curls were stuck damply to her forehead.

'Did Geri say how much longer?' I asked. Geri Paterson, head of the Medusa Project, was driving us to a training camp where we were going to have to stay – with no contact with our families – for six whole months.

'Another hour or so.' Ketty sighed.

I shook my head. Everything felt wrong. The journey was long and boring, sure. But I was in no hurry to reach the camp, either – the whole point of being sent there was to 'learn discipline through hard work' according to Geri. Goodness knows what that would be like. The thought of it filled me with horror. Physical activities are not exactly my strong point.

Nico emerged from the café. 'Depressed because you won't be going to school for half a year, Ed?' He put his arm round Ketty, a big grin on his face.

She beamed up at him. I turned away. I'm not going into it here, but a few weeks before, Ketty and I had dated a bit. Then Nico told her he liked her and now they were all over each other. As Dylan might say, it sucked *big time*.

Geri strode out of the café. It didn't look as though stopping for a break had improved her mood at all. She was posing as a parent/school liaison officer responsible for taking the four of us to the camp, but she didn't look like any parent I'd ever met. She jumped into the driver's seat, calling angrily for us to join her.

'Come *on.*'

We sat as before, Nico and Ketty in the back, Dylan on her own in the middle row of seats and me up front next to Geri. I get a bit car sick if I sit anywhere else.

Mind you, the next part of our journey was enough to make anyone puke. The road quickly disappeared and we started bumping over really rocky ground.

With a snarl, Dylan appeared from behind her oversized sunglasses and took out her headphones. 'When are we going to quit freakin' bouncing around?'

I closed my eyes. Geri was in a bad enough mood without Dylan provoking her further.

Geri sucked in her breath. 'May I remind you that if you four hadn't taken matters into your own hands on your last job, you wouldn't have to be here *at all*,' she snapped.

Behind me, Ketty sighed. Her brother, Lex, was the reason we'd gone off on our own before. The criminal we were investigating, Damian Foster, had been holding him captive and Ketty had been attempting to find out where he was. The rest of us were helping. I knew Ketty felt responsible for getting us all into trouble with Geri. I turned round and smiled at her. She smiled gratefully back.

'Just because you're sending us to some brat camp doesn't mean it has to be in the middle of nowhere,' Dylan snapped back, shoving her headphones back on.

'It's in the middle of nowhere for your own protection,'

Geri said. I glanced down at her hands, gripping the steering wheel. She was holding on so tightly that the knuckles were white. 'And may I remind you that I was up for *hours* last night finding a new camp after the original one was compromised.'

The atmosphere in the car chilled further. Geri had reminded us of this fact on average once every ten minutes since we started the journey.

'Yeah, you said,' Nico said sarcastically.

'This is *not* what I signed up for,' Geri muttered. 'I expected you all to behave . . . to do what I told you . . .'

I looked away. As usual I'd been lumped in with the others. It wasn't fair.

'We didn't sign up for any of this, either,' Nico muttered.

I could hear Ketty whispering in his ear, presumably telling him to calm down. I sighed. Nico was right, of course. None of us had chosen to be part of the Medusa Project – not the original gene implantation before we were born, nor the crime-fighting work we were being trained to do now. Geri was *forcing* us to work for her.

After another half-an-hour or so, with the sun hovering over the distant mountains, a long white building shimmered into view.

'Is that it?' I asked, leaning forward to see the place that was going to be our home from now until October.

'Yes, dear.' The sharp edges of Geri's bob batted her chin as she gave a vigorous nod. 'Camp Felicidad.' She raised her voice. 'Dylan, take those headphones out. I need to go over your final briefing.'

Grumbling, Dylan did so.

'What does Feliss-y-whatsit mean?' Ketty asked.

'Camp Lucky,' I translated. 'Hey, maybe the name's a good sign.'

Behind me, Dylan snorted. 'Yeah, right, Chino Boy.'

Dylan was always taking the mickey out of my clothes . . . out of me generally, in fact. Not that I cared, really.

As we drew nearer, Geri went through our cover stories again. We had each been assigned a new surname and background, part of which was that we'd all attended the same school. I was Ed Jones, bright but lazy – a formerly straight A student, who was now giving his wealthy parents a massive headache because he wanted to spend his days smoking weed instead of concentrating on his GCSEs.

'Remember, you're all the delinquent children of well-off, middle-class, concerned parents,' Geri cautioned. 'Like everyone else at the camp.'

'Oh good,' Dylan drawled. 'Six months with a bunch of spoilt brats . . . I can't wait.'

'Don't worry, Dyl,' Nico said. 'You'll fit right in.'

'Freakin' shut up,' Dylan snapped. 'And don't call me Dyl. It's bad enough going to some hell hole Brat Camp, without you starting on me.'

Geri just pursed her lips. 'Discipline . . . discipline,' she tutted.

The large white building was now identifiable as three separate houses. The biggest was in the centre – a low, sprawling concrete structure with small windows and a few thorny bushes by the front door. A man stood outside, arms folded.

'Camp Lucky's not very nice-looking, is it?' Ketty said, disappointed.

'It's not supposed to be,' Geri snapped. 'You're here to learn to behave yourselves. It's perfectly adequate, with a good record on discipline.'

Nico muttered something from the back of the jeep.

'Most importantly, it's safe. No-one here knows who you are, so you'll be able to lie low while we can make sure your identities are still secret from Damian Foster and Blake Carson and all the other criminals who'd give their eye teeth to get their hands on you.'

I gritted my teeth. The worst part of us being sent here was that, in the outside world, everyone apart from our parents thought we were dead. Geri had gone to extreme lengths over this. She'd exploded a bomb in our school, then changed all our records to say we'd died in the blast. She insisted this was necessary for our own protection but it made me angry – if Geri hadn't forced us to become the Medusa Project, we wouldn't *need* protecting.

Anyway, we were under strict instructions to keep our skills under wraps while we were at the camp. *That* I didn't have a problem with. I hate being able to mind-read. It's an invasion of privacy. It's *wrong*.

234

The jeep juddered over rough paving stone and came to a halt. I opened my eyes. We'd arrived. The man who'd been standing by the door was now advancing towards us, a big smile on his face. He looked very Spanish – dark hair and eyes and the same olive skin as Nico. He pulled open Geri's door and extended a hand to help her out. The hot air surged into the car like somebody had trained a hairdryer on us.

'Welcome to Camp Felicidad. You must be Ms Paterson.'

I stared at him. Apart from a slight nasal twang in his voice, the man could have been English.

'Welcome.' The man glanced round at the four of us. I quickly averted my eyes, not wanting to make eye contact and be forced to dive into his mind.

'Do any of you young people speak Spanish?' the man asked.

'Ed does,' Geri said, indicating me. 'And Dylan here's good at it too.'

Senor Fernandez looked at us expectantly.

'Hola,' Dylan said, sulkily.

'Como se llama usted?' I asked, trying to sound polite.

'You may call me Senor Fernandez,' the man replied. 'I hope your stay here will be fruitful. Now, I'm sure you're eager to get your bearings.' He stood back to make way for Geri and pointed towards the house. 'Beautiful ladies first.'

Geri smiled – one of those knowing smiles that basically mean the person knows they're being flattered but likes it anyway.

We followed the two of them into the house. It was still

steamily hot outside, despite the fact that the sun was so low in the sky. The contrast inside the house was startling. So cool I almost shivered. The thick stone walls clearly blocked out much of the heat. A fan blasted away in the corner. I blinked, taking in the stone flags on the floor, the reception desk in the corner and the long trestle table down the middle of the room.

'Looks like a hostel,' Ketty whispered in my ear. 'I was expecting worse from what Dylan said about brat camps.'

'This is where we eat.' Senor Fernandez indicated the table with a sweep of his hand. 'Our other young people are busy with evening chores. You'll meet them a little later.' He turned to Geri. 'Is it to your satisfaction so far, Ms Paterson?'

Geri gave him a brisk nod. 'It seems suitably basic,' she said. 'Though to be honest, dear, I don't care what it looks like, so long as these kids learn some discipline while they're here.'

Ketty and Nico exchanged exasperated glances behind Geri's back.

'Of course.' Senor Fernandez gave a little bow. He led us down a corridor to the girls' quarters – a six-bed dorm, much bleaker than the one back at Fox Academy. The walls were plain white – no posters or pictures. Each bed was covered with a pale blue quilt and stood next to a small locker. The tops of the lockers were completely clear.

Geri nodded approvingly.

'Clean and simple,' Fernandez said.

'. . . like a cell,' Nico muttered.

Senor Fernandez flashed a fierce look at him. 'Rule number one,' he snapped. 'Young people must ask for permission to speak.' His face relaxed. 'However, an adjustment period for new young people is only fair, so no de-merits tonight.'

'De- what?' Nico said.

Senor Fernandez shook his head and made a clicking sound at the back of his throat. He turned his attention back to Geri. 'The boys' room is identical, just in a different part of the building. Would you like to see that now?' he asked.

Geri hesistated, checking her watch. 'I really don't have time,' she said.

'Absolutely fine – of course, you need to get going.' Fernandez gestured back to the main lobby. 'Let me see you out.'

We left Dylan and Ketty in their room and followed Fernandez back down the corridor.

As we reached the lobby, Geri turned to me and Nico.

'Please use this as an opportunity to learn some discipline,' she said, with heavy emphasis. 'I'll call on the Camp phone one week from tonight to see how you're getting on.'

I nodded. Nico just stared sullenly at the floor.

'Right, well, goodbye, then.' She took a step towards the front door.

'Let me see you to your car, Ms Paterson,' Fernandez said. He turned to Nico and me. 'You two boys wait here. *Don't move.*'

Geri and Fernandez left. I sighed and looked round the room. The trestle table had been scrubbed so hard that the wood in the middle was almost white. The dresser behind was stacked with plates and glasses. There was no mess . . . nothing that made it feel homely at all.

'Ed.'

I spun round. Nico was standing beside the door on the far side of the room, beyond the long table. He opened it softly and peered round. 'Come on,' he said quietly. 'There's a corridor down here, with a door and a window.'

'*Nico,* for goodness sake.' My heart thudded. 'That man told us to stay here.'

'Lighten up, man,' Nico made a face. 'I'm just gonna take a quick look. I'll be back before Senor Fussypants knows we were gone.' He disappeared through the door.

Muttering angrily to myself, I crossed the room towards him. It was all very well Nico saying he was only taking a 'quick look'. If Fernandez came back and found him gone, I could just imagine how much trouble we would *both* be in.

I reached the door and peered round it. Nico was standing in a gloomy corridor, staring out of a window onto an empty, shaded courtyard.

'Come back,' I hissed.

Nico shook his head. 'We've got a second.' He frowned, still staring out at the courtyard. 'Where d'you think every-one is?' he whispered.

'Working, remember?' I said.

'Oh yeah. "The *young people* are doing their chores",'

238

Nico said, in a fair imitation of Fernandez' voice. 'Don't you hate being called that . . . young people? It's so patronising.'

'Nico, will you—'

'Jesus, man, *look!*' Nico held up his hand to silence me. '*Look,*' he repeated, pointing through the window. A line of five or six kids – some about our age, others younger – were crossing the bleak stone courtyard, following after a thick-set man with a snake tattoo down one of his arms.

The kids were dressed shabbily, though they looked clean. But there was something defeated about the way they were walking that sent a chill down my spine.

As we watched, one of the younger kids said something, and the man with the tattoo hit him across the head. The boy stumbled sideways, then carried on walking.

My mouth fell open. I moved closer to the window.

Nico sucked in his breath. 'That doesn't look like the *young people* doing their chores, does it?'

I shook my head, frowning.

We watched for a moment longer. As they reached the edge of the toilets in the centre of the courtyard, Tattoo Man struck another member of the group, a skinny girl with long dark hair. The girl fell to the ground. The man pointed to her trailing shoe lace and the girl knelt, meekly, to tie it.

'Jesus Christ,' Nico breathed. 'What *is* this place?'

I glanced back into the Camp lobby. The front door was still firmly shut. I caught the echo of Geri's high tinkly laugh in the distance. She and Fernandez must still be talking.

I took a deep breath and joined Nico by the window.

239

From here I could see the whole courtyard. It was paved with large stone slabs and flanked on one side by what looked like a barn and on the other by a white building similar in style to the main house. Apart from the toilets in the centre, where the kids were now lined up, the courtyard was empty.

As we watched, Tattoo Man and the other kids vanished round the side of the toilets, leaving the skinny dark-haired girl in plain view, still struggling with her shoe lace.

Nico darted down the corridor to the door that led onto the courtyard. He yanked on the handle. Locked. He raised his hand in the gesture he uses to perform telekinesis.

'What are you doing?' I said, appalled.

'Listen,' he said, urgently. 'If what we've just seen is typical of what goes on in this Camp, then we need to find out and tell Geri before she leaves.' He twisted his hand. There was a click as the lock undid and the door sprang ajar. I stared, impressed in spite of myself. I'd never tell him so, but Nico's telekinetic skills are pretty amazing to watch.

Nico pushed the door open and stepped into the courtyard.

I hesitated for a second, then followed.

The heat hit me hard. Even in the shade of the courtyard it was like stepping into an oven. I glanced round as we crept across the paving stones. No one at the windows. At least we wouldn't be spotted from inside the house.

Nico had already reached the girl. She jumped as he

240

touched her shoulder. He said something in a low voice while I ran past and peered round the side of the hut.

The other kids and Tattoo Man were gathered next to a ramshackle old VW bus, parked in the shade of a single tree. Next to the bus was a huge wooden well, with a fenced area beyond. This area was strikingly lush and green compared to the arid desert all around us. Tattoo Man was talking in Spanish. His speech was too rapid for me to catch any of the words, but he was clearly barking out orders.

I turned back to Nico and the girl.

'Que?' she was whispering. 'Quien eres?'

Nico turned to me. 'I don't understand what she's saying,' he whispered.

I barely heard him. I was staring at the girl, transfixed. I wasn't looking right into her eyes, obviously, but I'd already seen they were beautiful – a sea-green colour that stood out against her tanned skin. And it wasn't just her eyes. *She* was beautiful. About my age, with a worried, oval-shaped face, a long nose and silky dark hair that curled onto her shoulders.

'*Ed*,' Nico hissed.

'She asked who we were,' I explained.

'Ed,' I said to the girl. 'Me llamo Ed. Este es Nico. Y tu? Como te llamas?'

The girl was trying to look into my eyes, but I kept my gaze averted.

'Luz,' she whispered. 'Me llamo Luz. You . . . Eds, English . . . please, help . . .'

'What are you saying?' Nico hissed beside us.

'Just our names,' I said. 'She's called Luz.'

'Loos?' Nico said.

'Luz, donde eres?' Tattoo Man shouted from round the corner.

Luz froze. Nico grabbed my arm with one hand and Luz's with the other and dragged us into the WC marked *Senors* – the men's toilet.

We stood in the narrow, dimly-lit corridor. A stench drifted out from the toilets that had to be just around the tiled corner.

'Ask her what the hell's going on here,' Nico demanded.

A second later, a shadow fell across the doorway. I held my breath and pressed my back against the cool concrete wall.

'LUZ, ven aqui!' It was the man, even angrier than before. He swore in Spanish, then said something I just about understood about there not being time for a toilet break.

He thought Luz was in the ladies toilet next to this one.

Luz took a step towards the door. I grabbed her arm. I didn't dare speak in case the man heard us. If I wanted to know what was going on here, I was going to have to mind-read her. I pulled Luz round until she met my eyes.

In a second I was inside her mind. People always freak when that happens the first time, and Luz was no exception. Her mind was jumping around, full of fear and confusion. Mind you, my own thoughts were jumping about just as badly.

Hola, I stammered – not knowing what else to thought-speak. *It's okay. Who is that man?*

Que? Luz's mind was still all over the place, her thought-speech tumbling out.

How this? A single strand of thought stood out above the rest: *We must quick . . . Eds, English . . . you just come in camp, no?*

Si. I tried to make my mind settle.

This place no es good. Senor Fernandez es bad man. You go. Tell persons . . . help . . .

Where are you going in the van?

Que?

Donde vas en el . . . el coche grand?

Damn it, why did my Spanish have to desert me now?

No se . . . I don't know . . . Ed. Por favor. Ayudame.

Ayudame. Help me. My stomach turned over.

'Luz!' The man outside sounded very close. 'Are you in the *men's* toilet?' he said in Spanish.

Need go, Luz's thought-speech grew panicky. *Help.*

'Ed, leave it,' Nico hissed, right in my ear.

I will help, I promise. I broke the connection.

Luz burst through the door. We waited, holding our breath. I could hear the man yelling at her, then the slap of a hand, presumably making contact with Luz's head. I raged silently at the thought of her being hurt.

A few more seconds passed, then Nico peered after her. 'They've gone, come on,' he said.

He slipped outside and raced across the courtyard. I

followed, more slowly, a large part of me wanting to find Luz. I could hear the bus revving up round the corner.

What was happening to her? Where was she being taken?

And then a large hand clamped down on my shoulder and Senor Fernandez' heavy, nasal voice sounded in my ear.

'Only in camp five minutes,' he said, 'and you, Ed, are already in the deepest of deep shits.'

**The adventure continues in *The Rescue*,
coming soon!**

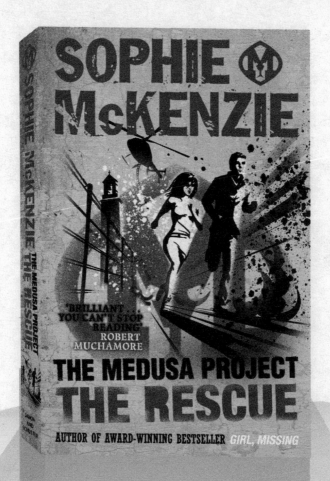

SOPHIE McKENZIE

'BRILLIANT
YOU CAN'T STOP
READING'
ROBERT
MUCHAMORE

THE MEDUSA PROJECT
THE RESCUE

AUTHOR OF AWARD-WINNING BESTSELLER *GIRL, MISSING*

Fourteen years ago, four babies were implanted
with the Medusa gene – a gene for psychic abilities.
Now teenagers, Nico, Ketty, Ed and Dylan together make
up The Medusa Project – a secret, government-funded,
crime-fighting force, currently in hiding from the
criminal underworld at a secret training camp. . .

THE THIRD EXCITING ADVENTURE!

"BRILLIANT ... YOU CAN'T STOP READING"— ROBERT MUCHAMORE

SOPHIE McKENZIE

THE MEDUSA PROJECT
THE SET UP

THE MEDUSA PROJECT
THE SET UP

AUTHOR OF AWARD-WINNING BESTSELLER *GIRL, MISSING*

Fourteen years ago, scientist William Fox implanted
four babies with the Medusa gene – a gene for psychic
abilities. Now those babies are teenagers – and unaware
that their psychic powers are about to kick in . . .

**READ THE FIRST EXCITING BOOK
IN THIS BRAND NEW
SOPHIE MCKENZIE SERIES!**

Are you who you *think* you are?

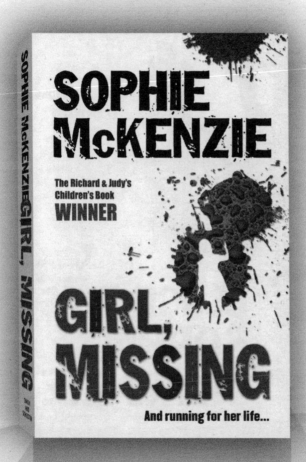

Lauren is adopted and eager to know about her
mysterious past. But when she discovers she may
have been snatched from another family as a baby,
her whole life is turned upside down...

Could *you*
be a clone?

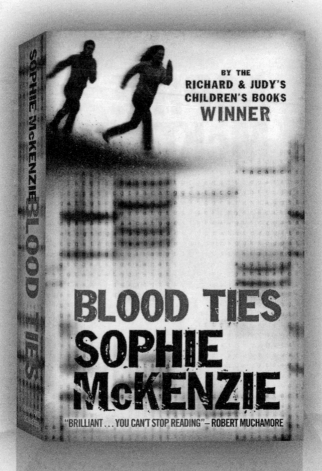

BY THE
RICHARD & JUDY'S
CHILDREN'S BOOKS
WINNER

SOPHIE McKENZIE BLOOD TIES

BLOOD TIES
SOPHIE McKENZIE

"BRILLIANT . . . YOU CAN'T STOP READING" – ROBERT MUCHAMORE

Linked by a firebombing at a research clinic,
Theo and Rachel fear they are targets of an
extremist group who will stop at nothing to
silence them – and who know more about
their true identities than they do . . .